She Wore A Sky Blue Ribbon

By

Paul Gilbert

To the Sky Blue Army.

Safe journey home
and away.

Dedication

This book is dedicated to the people of Coventry.

She Wore A Sky Blue Ribbon

Steve knew Sarah was out of his league

And Coventry City had drawn Man United in the FA Cup.

So things were grim. What chance did they have?

In January 1987 temperatures were sub-zero and the outlook was bleak, but at eighteen Steve had the world at his feet and his eye on a girl. She was in a different class, but he could make her laugh and that was half the battle.

He went home and away with Coventry City and there was something about them that year. They had a happy-go-lucky attitude that brought results and no matter who they played, they fancied their chances...

...Tottenham or Chelsea. United or anyone.

And when your name is on the Cup, anything is possible.

So if dreams can come true, why not dream big? What was he scared of?

The worst thing that could happen is painful heartbreak...

...but maybe 1987 is going to be his year?

Everyone loves the romance of the Cup and everyone loves an underdog, even if not all your dreams come true.

A Story of George and John's Sky Blue Army. Go For It!

Looking Back

Heaven isn't signposted.

You can't just go there

But it does exist.

What I call heaven is where your wildest dreams come true.

Like Wembley Stadium on the 16th of May 1987.

I'd been on the journey and I didn't really believe it was going to happen, even as we got closer and closer. Right up until the last moment, I was convinced it would be snatched away.

And when it happened, it changed my life.

I learned dreams can come true, even the impossible ones that you daredn't even say out loud.

I learned that heaven was out there, one of life's possibilities, so you've got to keep the faith.

And I learned that if, like me, your heaven is being with another person, then it helps if that person's heaven is being with you.

CHAPTER ONE

Saturday January 10th 1987

The terraced-houses of Heath Street in Ball Hill did away with gardens in favour of a rock solid doorstep and an 'in your face' front door. This is helpful if, like me, you're in the delivery business, particularly when it's not been above freezing all day.

The last few days had been the coldest on record, not getting above minus five even in the afternoon. The treacherous ice that covered the road is two weeks old and not going anywhere anytime soon.

People said I must be crazy to start a Video Delivery Service and tonight I think they might be right, but here I am, the Saturday-night movie man, bringing VHS home-entertainment directly to you. I've got a white van with 'Movies To You' in graffiti-style letters spray painted on the side, and beneath that our Mission Statement 'Bringing the Magic of Video To Your Door'.

And it's mine. Just one of the business ventures I've started since I left school two years ago.

Whereas ice-cream vans play jaunty jingles and nursery rhymes, we have The Housemartins 'Caravan Of Love' on a boom-box turned up to ten.

As I pull up at our chosen spot, Andy hits play and in seconds the front doors are spewing out kids in their coats, hats, scarves. It's like Willy Wonka's dishing out free Wonka bars.

Andy doesn't seem too excited about it, but he can be hard to read sometimes. Although we were at junior school together, he looks a lot older than me. He's already got the look of the head-bouncer at Tomango's; the shaven-headed, six foot tall and five foot wide with a thousand-yard stare fine-tuned from playing semi-pro rugby. Andy loved rugby because, unlike playing football, 'you get a good punch-up and afterwards have a friendly drink and a laugh'. He's harder than a turtle's tit, but as soft as anything and the best mate anyone could ask for.

Most impressively, he only wears a T-shirt and a Harrington jacket in the freezing cold.

"Number eighteen has two returns from last Friday," I told him. "I suspect there may be a need for some conflict-resolution."

Andy nodded and we stepped out of the relative warmth of the van and into the gale-force wind and sub-zero cold.

Heath Street, long and straight, disappeared to a vanishing point in both directions. It's all two-up-two-down houses and salt of the earth people, with a few bad apples thrown in. A case in point being my friend at number eighteen.

The house wasn't exactly screaming out 'pride of ownership'. The door's peeling paintwork revealed damp hardboard beneath. The top section's glass panels were a mosaic of coloured cardboard, which couldn't be doing much in the way of insulation and beneath that a plastic number '1' clung on next to the shadow of a departed '8'. It couldn't even be bothered to fit the frame that it was designed to prevent entry to, it just kind of lay in place with gaps everywhere. Pretty shoddy stuff, in all honesty.

Despite its frailty, I gave the door three solid whacks with the side of my fist, producing three pleasingly dull thuds.

I turned back to the van where six kids were jostling for position, waiting for Andy to throw open the doors. Each one was bouncing on the soles of their feet as the moment of choosing their evening's video entertainment approached. Once Andy opened the doors, the scramble got serious. This is survival of the fittest in action and Darwin would have laughed his duck off. If they weren't quick, they'd be watching The Muppets Takes Manhattan with their little sister instead of Die Hard or Aliens, like the cool kids. The video racks were all within arm's reach, but some kids had shorter arms than others. The winning technique was to scan the huge rack of movies on offer and spot good targets in that very same instant. Then it was a mad scramble, limbs reaching and flailing. Andy stepped back and put his hands in his jeans pocket, his only concession to the cold and the rain.

Voices shriek at the finding of treasure.

"Commando!"

"Indiana Jones!"

"Seen it!"

A mum appeared at the side of the van, pulled her parka around her chest with one hand and clung to her cigarette with the other.

"Don't hang about," she instructed her offspring, "I'm bloody freezing." Her voice had the sweetness of gravel sliding off a shovel.

Andy nodded to the young lady who smiled back, her top lip creased with smoker's lines.

The first victor, a wiry dark-haired girl, emerged, clutching her chosen VHS.

"How much is this one?" she asked, taking the copy of Beverley Hills Cop from him.

Andy said, "A pound for two nights."

"It's not much good to me, is it? I can't stand all that fighting and blood and guts."

"Well, you can't win 'em all," Andy consoled her.

She said, "Have you got anything else on offer?"

Andy raised an eye-brow as she let cigarette smoke drift from her lips.

"Second one's half price," I told her from the door step of number eighteen.

She nodded her approval and took another drag.

"What do you like? Comedy or romance?" I asked her.

She smiled. "I like anything. I'm not fussy. And I see loads of bloody comedy around here, but not much romance."

"Well, you can't go wrong with the new Police Academy."

"Which one is it?"

"Three!"

She nodded. "Yeah OK."

Andy braved the mob of children storming the van, retrieved Police Academy 3, and handed it to her. "There you go, love."

"Ain't you cold?" she asked, eyeing that T-shirt that stretched across his chest.

"Don't forget popcorn, crisps, chocolate, all in date or near enough," I shouted to the kids. "The second one's half-price."

More kids appeared with their mums or older sisters and soon hustled Andy with their selections. We were coining in the money now. It was a feeding frenzy, like those traders on the stock exchange floor or a bookie at the track before a big race. He'd never admit, but I knew Andy loved being the video-delivery-man. We made people happy. Gave them what they wanted. Films were hired and returned and somehow none went missing, or very few.

Speaking of which, the occupant of number eighteen was taking his time to answer the door.

I knocked again, even firmer this time, and gave him a few more seconds. Then, through the murky stained glass, something approached. The door opened. He had a nasty face on him, but it's forced. There weren't any scars, bumps, or war wounds. He's a bully. I hate bullies.

"We don't want nothing," he said. The stains on his once-white vest were overlapping, stains upon stains. I count three different shades where his beer belly started.

He tried to shut the door, but I reached out a hand and stopped it an inch before it hit the frame. This ain't my first time dealing with a problem customer.

Affronted, he yanked the door back open and stepped forward. He did his best irate frown, but it's a poor performance, like bad acting in an even worse pantomime, which is exactly what he was. It might work on his wife and kids, but not on me.

He started off, "I said-"

"I heard what you said," I told him, "but you didn't allow me to retort."

That frown stayed stuck to his face. "We don't want nothing."

"Maybe not, but you have to return the films you rented from me last week."

"I didn't have nothing last week. You have the wrong house."

He pushed the door shut, but it rebounded off my foot, which I'd planted on the door-frame.

"You had 'Last House On The Left' and 'The Burning' and paid one pound fifty, taking advantage of our generous 'second movie half-price' offer. You may remember, we were chatting by the van about our respective New Year's festivities. You got shit-faced in the Royal Oak, as I recall. Does that jog any memories?"

"You think you're smart, don't ya?"

"Well, I do have a good memory, particularly in my business dealings, which is not necessarily a good indicator of intelligence, but it does mean I can recall certain facts, such as, you got my video cassettes and I want them back. Now!"

"My kids lost 'em," he said.

"Really?"

He nodded and shrugged. Check-mate, game-over. Loser.

"That's a bit careless," I said.

"Well, I don't have your crappy films, so what you gonna do about it?"

"Me?" I said, "I'm not gonna do nothing about it, that's not my department."

I turned to the van where Andy was serving the last customer. I raise an arm and Andy eyeballed the stained-vest guy and gave a sinister nod.

"Repossession is his department," I explained. "He's good at it too. You know, between you and me, he takes it all a bit too serious. He won't listen to anyone. Even I can't reason with him when it comes to repossessing video cassettes. He's like a dog with a bone. Or is it a bull in a china shop? Could be both actually."

I laughed, but the number eighteen guy didn't see the funny side.

"They're rental quality video-cassettes and retail at sixty quid each, so he'll accept goods of an equal value. He does insist on doing his own valuations, though, but as I say, he's very fair. It will be a hundred and twenty quids' worth of your stuff and not a penny more."

He watched as Andy served the last customers and then adjusted the sovereign rings on first his right hand, then his left.

The vest-guy's nostrils flared. He glared at me. His check-mate thwarted.

"Wait here," he said, and retreated into the dark depths of his pokey abode.

Back at the van, I slotted number eighteen's returned movies back into the horror section and slammed both double doors shut.

Heath Street was our last stop. The cold beginning to seriously bite.

I dropped into the driver's seat and fished the keys out of my pocket despite the numbness of my fingers.

"How was the City game?" Andy asked, cupping his hands in front of his mouth and blowing visible breath through his fingers.

"Anti-climax," I said.

Coventry City had beaten Bolton in the third round of the FA Cup. It was never going to be a life-changing event, but if we'd lost, it would've ruined a perfectly average post-New Year's weekend.

"Playing a third division team is always a worry, so I did fear the worst. And the pitch was frozen over, so it was like playing on an ice-rink covered in banana-skins. But by fifteen minutes we're two-nil up and by half-time we were three-nil up and it's all over. What was I worried about? But then the second-half was a waste of time. The players were freezing, the fans were even more freezing and no one wanted to be there. I was bored-shitless."

"That's life as a Cov fan," Andy said. "We always fear the worst. If we all supported Liverpool, then life would be one long Champions party."

"Be a plastic scouser?" I said. "No thanks."

There was a time, although briefly, when I was almost coerced into becoming a Liverpool fan. I was nine years old and my uncle, a dyed-in-the-wool plastic Liverpool fan, had bought me a red and white scarf. He also laced the present with a promise and a prediction, 'We're going to win the League this season, you'll see!'

And, ironically, it was that scarf and the Third Round of the FA Cup tie against lower league opposition that started my love affair with Coventry City ten years ago. It was January 8th, 1977 at Highfield Road against Millwall.

My dad decided that supporting anyone other than your hometown team is not something he wanted for his son and so, on the morning of the match, he announced we were going to watch Coventry City. I was excited, but didn't really know what to expect.

Confusingly, my dad had emptied his wicker fishing basket.

"For you to stand on," he'd explained.

I was nine years old and loved my football, but that translated to kicking a small plastic ball around the school playground and fanatically collecting Panini stickers and bubblegum cards with every bit of spare cash I could scrape together.

Outside there was snow on the ground and the temperature was freezing.

"You need to wear a scarf," my mum ordered once we declared we were ready to leave.

We were in the kitchen. I had my big-coat on over a woolly jumper, long football socks underneath my jeans and a black bobble hat pulled down to cover my ears.

"I don't have a scarf," I shrugged.

"You have that red one," she corrected me.

"That's Liverpool!" I told her, "We're going to watch Coventry!"

My dad coughed and something unspoken passed between him and mum.

He knelt down to my level and pulled up the collar of my coat. "You can wear the red one, can't you, Steve?"

I frowned at them both for being so unfair.

My mum's response was to retrieve the inappropriate scarf from the cupboard under the stairs and to offer it to me.

"Wear the scarf or stay at home," she said, "Your choice."

I was furious, but took the scarf.

We parked in one of the streets near Highfield Road. The floodlights were already on, creating a white and yellow glow above the houses. It filled me with an expectation of the unknown, like we were going to see an alien landing or some kind of prison camp.

Hundreds of people, mostly men, were swarming alongside us. My dad took my hand and as we turned the corner of Nicholls Street and onto Thackhall Street, I saw the Highfield Road Stadium for the first time. The Sky Blue Stand and West Stand were magnificent structures, rising from the ground like enormous open theatres, and towering high above them stood the four floodlight towers that hurt my eyes, but I couldn't stop staring at them.

Dad paid at the turnstile, 'One adult, one child', and ushered me in. I pushed through the rotating gate until it clicked behind me. Dad followed me, the empty fishing basket strapped over his shoulder.

"Are you ready for this?" he asked me.

I nodded, but I didn't really know what I was ready for, except that it was something amazing.

Dad took my hand and we climbed up the concrete steps that led to the Sky Blue terrace. It was then that I first set my eyes on the beautifully illuminated green grass and white lines of the pitch.

"There it is, son," dad said. "The hallowed turf of Highfield Road."

I'd never seen anything like it. And I didn't know what hallowed meant, still don't, but it certainly looked hallowed.

I stopped in my tracks and stared at the playing field, the white lines, the goalposts and the nets. I knew right then such a place existed for gladiators and warriors to do battle. Opposite us was another monumental structure, the Main Stand, populated by people on wooden seats and to our left the open expanse of the Spion Kop.

We picked a spot beside the tall steel fence that separated the Sky Blue Terrace and the West End. Dad dropped the fishing basket down and I climbed onto it and held onto the fence.

He put his arm around my back and said, "You alright, Stevey?"

I nodded. I was very much alright.

I checked that I'd tucked my Liverpool scarf out of sight beneath my collar and I was ready.

The crowd filled up and the noise levels escalated in anticipation. I was taking it all in, as much as I could, and then, as the crowd rumble became a roar, my dad pointed to the tunnel opposite us as the two teams emerged.

Something wasn't right, though.

Millwall were wearing their away shirts of all white, but Coventry, although at home, were also playing in their away kit.

"Must've been a colour clash," my dad said, thinking aloud.

I wasn't listening.

I pulled my red scarf out from under my coat and proudly raised it above my head. The only red scarf amongst the seventeen thousand Coventry City fans that matched their changed red kit. The West End was a sea of sky blue and white scarves see-sawing above the heads of the fans as the teams lined up. It was an awesome sight. I felt part of it, but also unique in my own contribution to the whole. This was the feeling I always got from football, being part of a crowd but never more of like an individual at the same time.

In goal, Jim Blyth 'kept us in the game' with some great saves and my dad said that we were 'missing Fergie up front'. He was injured. I had this mystical Mick Ferguson figure in my football card collection and he looked like a beast of a man with wild eyes and a huge, bushy beard. I wondered what horrific injury could to prevent this ogre from playing.

We won one-nil. Bobby McDonald scored the only goal in the second half.

There were more people in Highfield Road that day than I had ever seen in one place, and it was my first experience of being in Sky Blue heaven. After saluting the team at the end, me and my dad headed home amongst the happy fans who were laughing and joking and swearing and smoking. This, I realised, was how a man should spend his Saturday afternoons; cheering on Tommy Hutchison, Mick Coop, Terry Yorath, Barry Powell, John Beck, Alan Green, and Les Cartwright.

The Sky Blues.

I was in love.

On that day I became a Coventry City fan.

My dad, sensing that I was taking this addiction seriously and seeing a need to manage my expectations, told me they don't always win and more often than not, they lose.

"Can we go every week?" I responded.

He laughed. "We'll see."

I have my dad to thank for doing the right thing by me. If he hadn't taken me that day, I'm sure things would've been different.

Driving to an auction in Devon that summer, he had a heart attack and died. I didn't understand when mum told me. I kept asking when he would come home. It sounds stupid, but it was only after the funeral that it hit me.

He wasn't coming home.

Dad taught me a lot, some of which meant little at the time, but it all made sense as I got older.

And he was right, we didn't always win and, more often than not, we did leave disappointed. Like most love-affairs, I wouldn't have it any other way because the rare good days made up for the many bad ones.

And, after all, we had won today and were in the draw for the fourth round.

I started the van and turned to Andy.

"It would be good if we had a cup-run, we are playing alright this season. Greg Downs scored from a free-kick, a twenty-five-yard screamer, Big Cyril's doing the business up front, rounded the keeper for the second, and their keeper gifted Dave Bennett the third."

"Bennett is a class player, but he'd be even better if he chased defenders like he chases women in Carey's," Andy said.

"If we get an easy draw next round," I pondered, "who knows after that?"

"You're dreaming," Andy said, then stated a simple law of physics, "Coventry City go downhill after New Year's Day. It happens every year without fail."

He had a point.

"You may be right, but sometimes you've got to think big."

"Says the guy who rents ropey videos to single-mothers and low-lives," Andy laughed.

"What do you mean?"

"Look around," he said, "what kind of customers do you expect when you cast your line around places like this? How you going to think big round here? Start selling packets of Rizla and Old Holburn as a side-line?"

"What's wrong with people round here?"

"There's nothing wrong with people round here Steve, but they've got no money."

"That's not their fault," I told him.

"I know, but you're the entrepreneur. Figure it out," he said. "If you want to go big, you gotta go upmarket."

In the three months since our launch, I'd intentionally stayed away from posh areas. My logic was that they had better things to do for their weekends' entertainment.

And I was sure that my cheeky-working-class-patter wouldn't work on the well-lit porches of their detached houses, with three cars on the drive.

Their money and status intimidated me, and though I'd never admit it under pain of death, I was jealous of what they had. I wanted that big house, flash car and holidays in Spain, as long as I got it under my own terms. And before my time ran out.

"You're right!" I said. "And that's exactly what I'm going to do. Come on, time to take things up a level!"

"Where are we going?" Andy asked.

"Well, if you're gonna go up market, then you gotta go big!" I said, pushing my foot down as the van roared down Heath Street, "We're going to Cannon Park."

< < < <   > > > >

I read the street sign out loud to hear how it sounds, "Riverdale Close."

"I know you said upmarket, but this is off the scale. Look at it," Andy said. He sounded overwhelmed despite instigating this seismic shift in my business strategy.

He had a point, though. I hadn't even known they had houses like these in Coventry. And Riverdale Close wasn't even an actual street, it was a group of enormous houses set in quarter acre blocks of manicured gardens, square-cut hedge, lush green lawns and gravel drives big enough for three coaches to park end-to-end. Fir trees and white picket fences were the only other garden features allowed. They didn't even permit ice here. Someone had put down some salt and done a decent job of clearing the whole road and even the road itself was posh, high-quality bricks perfectly aligned like a roman mosaic. Not a patch of concrete or pot hole in sight.

Also, there was no pavement. Pedestrians were clearly not encouraged, would certainly not be provided with a safe area to walk on and were fair game to be ran-over by concerned residents.

"I think these people probably have their evening's entertainment already arranged, mate," Andy sighed.

I reminded myself that Andy was less invested in 'Movies To You' as I was. He'd offered to help me out, temporarily, until I found a reliable customer base that didn't need a 'repossession specialist', but that had been three months ago. He got paid not much more than beer money, but he probably had better things to do with his Saturday evenings.

I was about to suggest that he wait in the van and let me do the legwork and the sales-pitch, but he was already out of the door with a lets-get-this-over-with swagger and I didn't have the heart to oppose him.

"I'll do this side," I shouted back to him, and headed up the driveway of Number One Riverdale Close.

The open porch was not much smaller than my bedsit and had lavish potted plants placed everywhere that somehow hadn't been nicked.

I knocked on the door and was immediately blinded by a 600-watt strip-light that turned the night into day.

I shielded my eyes and waited, but the door didn't open.

Instead, a voice asked, "What do you want?"

"Hi," I called back to the person behind the door. "You have a wonderful house! My name is Steve and I am the owner of Movies To You. We are a mobile video entertainment provider-"

"No, thank you," the voice interrupted, and the light went out. It sounded pretty final to me.

I moved on to the house next door.

Number Three opened the door but closed it again when I got to the 'we are a mobile video provider'.

Number Five was out and Number Seven threatened to call the police.

Standing proudly at the end was Number Nine Riverdale Close, the flagship house of the street.

The light brown gravel of the driveway crunched beneath my feet. I wondered if I'd triggered any alarms or land mines.

It was a mock-Tudor mansion. The bottom story was brickwork and the second storey was white rendering and dark brown woodwork. The tiled roof had three gable-end windows. At first glance, I thought it was two semi-detached houses but, of course, such a place would have been ceremonially burnt to the ground by the Riverdale Nazi-Party or Residents' Association. At the centre stood the enormous front door and covered porch. To the left were bay windows bigger than Owen Owen's, and, to the right, not one, but two garage doors.

The garden itself was a bigger replica of its neighbours, but had the audacity to have sculpted the perimeter hedge into separate blocks. It looked like the entrance and exit to a maze.

On the driveway were a blue BMW M5, a red two-seater Toyota MR2 and a Golf GTi Mk2 in grey. All this year's E-reg plates. Very nice. Andy was right. Our offer of cheap video rental was not going to be enough to tempt the owners of these automobiles away from whatever Saturday night entertainment they had already planned.

But I'd come this far and one more rejection wasn't going to hurt.

As I approached the front door, I glanced back to see Andy climb back in the van. I guessed he had (unsuccessfully) canvassed the other side of the street already, so Number Nine was the last-chance-saloon.

The front door opened.

The girl who answered had long brown hair, like Cindy Crawford, a pink lipstick smile, dark blue eyeliner and deep brown eyes. She wore a baggie red zip-up jacket with a huge Adidas logo up one arm and red trackie-bottoms and all-white Reebok high top trainers, the thick laces bowed on the top of her feet, not using the top two eyelets.

Here was an Adidas-angel.

What was she doing in Coventry?

And she was stunningly beautiful. I mean, there's no other way of saying it. The girl was breath-taking.

"Hi," I managed, my tongue twisting in my mouth like it was glued to a corkscrew. "You have a wonderful house!"

She slid her hands into the pockets and tilted her head as I spoke. Her smile was like genuine, she was adoring a puppy doing something cute. "My name is Steve and I am the owner of Movies To You. We are a mobile video provider-"

And she frowned as she repeated, "A mobile video provider? Nice idea. I like it."

Her accent was English, but sometimes she sounded American. Like she pronounced the word 'mobile' like it rhymed with 'no bull', like 'Mobil'.

I nodded. "We're a local provider that deliver films to your house, that's my van," I said and although it was the only van in Riverdale Close, I qualified the statement by adding, "The white one."

"So it is," she commented, and her smile gave way to a giggle. "Someone's spray-painted it."

"Yeah, that was me," I said, without realising she was reporting suspected vandalism. "It's our logo."

My brain was struggling to keep up. I couldn't believe how beautiful she was. That alone was too much to comprehend, and there was barely enough brain power left for conversation. It was like I'd stepped into a Hollywood Brat Pack movie.

Hoping that Andy was on the ball, I put my thumb and first finger to my lips and gave a fairly impressive high-pitch whistle.

As good as gold, he reversed the van up to us at the front door.

"Would you like to look through our titles?" I asked. "As you can see, when we say 'to your door', we mean it!"

She laughed again.

It was incredible.

"I'm actually really glad you found me. I need cheering up," she said, "and I love watching movies all night."

"Glad I can help!" I told her, thinking what a sweet invitation that would have been but clearly wasn't. "I'm sure we'll have something you'll love."

She looked at me and flashed that smile again. "Do you have The Goonies."

"It just so happens that we do," I said, and opened the doors to the van with a flourish. I flicked on the light, illuminating hundreds of VHS boxes and what was left of the popcorn and crisps.

I was sure that The Goonies would be there because we'd had it since November and hardly anyone one had rented it. I found it and handed it over.

"Thank you," she said, and her eyes lit up as she studied the cover.

"I always stock new releases, but have loads of classics too."

She looked up at me and nodded. "I'm impressed. You seem to know what you're doing."

She flicked through the rack, then she reached out and added Alien and Mona Lisa to The Goonies.

She clutched the three cassettes to her chest and turned back to me.

"So do I get a membership card or something?"

I shook my head, "We operate on a trust system."

"So you trust me already?" she said, sounding American again.

"One hundred percent," I said.

She nodded again. She seemed to be enjoying this.

"Besides, I know where you live," I said, narrowing my eyes. "So I know where to find you."

"What if I skip the country?" she said. "I might join the international jet-set."

I didn't doubt her. Those high-top Reeboks weren't from Joe Davis Sports.

"Like I say, I trust you," I said. "And I think you'll be very satisfied with our service."

"How much do I owe you?" she said.

"Well, tonight's your lucky night because we have an introductory offer. Your first three films are free," I said. "Our strategy is to get you hooked so you become a long-term customer."

"Thank you so much," she paused, then said, "I guess I should let you get back to work."

I wanted to say 'No, no it's fine, you're my last customer, I'm free for the rest of the evening'.

Instead, I said, "No problem, I'll pick them up on Monday evening if that's OK."

"I'll be here," she said.

"And would you like to take part in our customer feedback program? It's a three-minute questionnaire about how satisfied you are with Movies To You. Comments and suggestions will improve our service."

"Quite the entrepreneur, aren't you? Customer service? Feedback questionnaire?"

"Customer feedback is critical in all of my businesses."

"I'm impressed."

I smile, but say nothing.

"Alright then," she said.

"Yeah, thanks, I'll see you Monday night."

Then she stopped and said, "By the way, I'm Sarah."

"I'm Steve-" I said and got cut off by a long blast on a car horn. Then another.

Andy climbed out of the van, gave the driver an inquisitive look, and the tooting stopped.

"Oh, I gotta go," Sarah said. "Nice to meet you."

"Likewise," I said, "Enjoy the films."

"I will," she called.

She disappeared behind the front door, cradling my videos in her arms.

"Bye mum," she shouted into the house and someone called back, "Bye, love. See you later."

She reappeared wrapped in an acid stonewashed denim jacket with a fur-lined collar and closed the heavy front door behind her.

As she passed me, she gave me a coy, "Sorry, bye."

I smiled.

I followed her down the drive and got into the van.

The offending horn had come from a brand new red Audi Quattro. The driver, with an immaculate wedge hair cut, mid-twenties, was so full of himself that he hardly paid Sarah any attention as she got into the passenger seat.

"What a dickhead," I said to Andy. I suddenly felt cold again.

"A rich dickhead, though," Andy said.

"All flash and no class," I assured him.

"Look mate," Andy said, "It was a nice try. I particularly liked the 'when we say to your door we mean it' line, that was quality." Then added, "But these people live in a different world, and they don't open the door to outsiders. Especially not the likes of us."

Sarah looked back at us as the Audi reversed down the drive and I thought for a second she was going to wave, but then she thought better of it.

I caught her eye and gave her a wave and a wide smile and hoped that Quattro-boy was watching.

"Steve, you're breaking the laws of nature and you will be punished for it."

"What are you talking about?"

"You don't know these people," he said. "They're not like us. We're disposable to them, cannon fodder. They march us out of the trenches to overheat the enemy's machine guns and find land mines."

"I bet she goes to a public school."

Andy sighed. "You're not listening to me. Do not fall in love with anyone around here. Anywhere but here. Heath Street is better than here. These people are ruthless."

"She didn't look that ruthless to me. She's probably from a really nice family."

"Then how come they live here?"

"Maybe they worked their way up from-"

"And, by the way," Andy said, "since when did you do Free Introductory Offers?"

"Have you ever seen anyone like her?"

"Mate, you'll be a lamb to the slaughter. You do know that, don't you? They'll burn you at the stake for their own entertainment."

CHAPTER TWO

Sunday 11th January 1987

The following days were so slow that it was actually painful, and by that I mean that the passing of time caused me physical pain. I ached to see her again.

I tried to keep busy with business and looking for new projects to work on. I was always looking for more ways of generating income without being too consuming of my time.

My business plan was in its growth/expansion stage. The intention was to build my financial base with as many sources of income as were manageable. I had some capital, money left for me by my dad's life insurance, and I had to put it to good use.

My dad was a bit of a wheeler dealer. He bought and sold stock and merchandise in bulk, buying from manufacturers or importers and selling to market traders, shops and business owners. Known as an innovative businessman, he found new ways of working. He worked long hours and spent a lot of his time on the road, but he always made sure weekends were for family. Every Saturday we'd be doing something, even if it was just spending Saturday 'up town' in the precinct, toy shopping in Woolworths, lunch in the Wimpey, and ice cream in Broadgate to watch Peeping Tom sneaking a perv at Lady Godiva. 'Mucky bugger!' he'd say. Of course, we'd do the rounds in the market too, lots of hand-shaking and quiet words, nods and winks.

On Sundays he'd take me out, kicking a football in the park or visiting relatives, but mostly to 'get out from under mum's feet' so that she could cook Sunday dinner.

And he may have been a wheeler-dealer, but he was totally solid with money. Every month, he paid the mortgage, cleared the bills, savings topped up. And he made a point of telling me, 'make sure that money knows who's in charge or it will run off with the circus'.

What he didn't tell me was that he also took out a hefty life-insurance policy to look after mum 'if anything should happen' and to set aside something for me.

I learned all this from my mum years after he died when I was sixteen.

'A King's Ransom', as my mother had said when she broke that news to me. "He's trusted you with this, Stevey. This is for your future."

I certainly wasn't going to waste it. I was going to make sure my dad would've been proud of me. Every penny spent was scrutinised, and every deal worked down to the finest detail to get the most for my money. Andy would say I was tighter than a camel's arse in a sandstorm, but that's how it has to be when you're spending someone else's money.

I was always on the look-out for opportunities, keeping an eye on the streets and an ear to the ground, looking for the right place at the right time and then making things happen. I also stayed close to 'people', 'customers' who didn't even realise they were customers until I showed them what they needed.

Finding the next 'big thing' was one thing, finding the people who needed it was another. Calculator watches, Rubik's cubes, "Frankie Say" T-shirts, Slush Puppies, Sony Walkman rip-offs, leg-warmers and BMX bikes were all needed by people, once it was pointed out to them. The list goes on and it always will. Knowing who people were and what they needed and putting the two together was like connecting the power cables to the lightning bolt that sent Marty into the future.

To keep things ticking over, I made a mental note to go to the wholesaler with my mum on her next visit. She'd pick up cleaning supplies and I would pick up anything that I could sell on the video round or anywhere else. Chocolate, popcorn, but I was thinking maybe perfume or something as a 'special', or The Pink.

My one 'serious' ex-girlfriend, Annie, could never understand why I couldn't get a 'normal job' like everyone else. We saw each other for six months. She dumped me after I explained in no uncertain terms that I would never work for anyone else. Never. And that's how it is. I wasn't too heartbroken, and I knew she did the right thing. We were very different people. She would later tell Andy she thought I was selling drugs, but maybe she made that up after the break-up.

< < < <   > > > >

I went out that Saturday night. I met Andy and Chris in the Tally Ho at ten and talked them into going to Park Lane, which was a rarity for me but I wanted something to kill the pain and you never know who might be in there.

We queued for thirty minutes. Larking about in the cold was a laugh.

Chris was going on, as always, about Karen, who he'd been going out with since he was thirteen and we were all at school together.

Andy was telling us about all the aggro at his work. He was on a YTS scheme at Courtaulds.

"There's this one lad I cannot stand," Andy was explaining.

Andy was a gentle-giant until you pissed him off. So I had an idea how this story was going to end up, but the enjoyment was in the telling.

"And he's seen some Bruce Lee movie or something and so he's made these steel throwing stars in the metal-workshop and ground the tips down to sharp points. These things are deadly and he's throwing them into the walls and stuff, and he turns to me from about four feet away and says 'Don't move' and he aims at my foot.

"I'm like, 'You what?' And he says again, 'Don't move'. So I say, 'You better throw it now or you'll look like a right prick' and he bottles it going, 'Nah, you'll flinch' and I tell him 'I've never flinched in my life mate'. So now he's looking more nervous than a pregnant nun on bath-night and I'm snarling at him, saying 'Go on, throw it then!' and he goes to throw but he's shaking like a shitting dog."

Andy was a big fan of the simile.

"Did he throw it?" I asked.

"What do you think?"

Needless to say, the outcome wasn't too favourable for the adventurous star-thrower who had been spared serious harm, but been forced to issue an humiliating public apology.

Inside the club, I spoke to a few people and arranged a few things, but my heart wasn't into the whole socialising thing. I met a few old mates, acquaintances, drank some overpriced water laced with lager, and nodded my head on the dance floor for a while. The whole time I was constantly looking around, scrutinising the face of every girl with long brown hair, but each time I was disappointed.

She wasn't there.

I kept telling myself: She could walk through the door at any moment. It was Park Lane on a Saturday night in Coventry. Where else would she go?

Somewhere else, apparently.

Just knowing she was out there was the most exhilarating feeling, and at the same time it was the worst.

What if she was madly in love with the Audi Quattro guy?

What if they were, like, soul-mates?

What chance would I have?

I began to wish I hadn't met this girl and that things would be as they were.

If Andy hadn't pushed me to 'think big', and if I hadn't decided to go 'up market' and if we'd taken the nest turn past Riverdale Close, or the one before it, then I wouldn't have known any different. Tonight would have been a normal Saturday night. My world would be full of opportunities and possibilities because ignorance is bliss. And there are many worse things in the world than bliss.

But now I had just one opportunity, one possibility.

Nothing else mattered.

A different world had revealed itself and whispered in my ear, 'This is how good your life could be!' then it added, 'Or not' and shrugged. Who knows?

And it was killing me.

Once the DJ started with the Whitney Houston stuff, I said my goodbyes to Chris and Andy and slipped away.

I walked back to the bedsit. It was freezing.

Each second and every step hurt bad, but I told myself that each tick of the clock was one step closer to the future. One step closer to Monday night.

Maybe I'd feel different in the morning, back to my old self.

The bedsit was above the Taj Mahal restaurant between the guitar shop and the Joke Shop in Whitefriars Street. Opposite was the Colin Campbell pub, which I never went in, and the Theatre One Cinema was just around the corner. 'The Taj' belonged to a relative of a friend of my mum, Mr Chandra. The bedsit was no more than a room next to a bathroom on the disused top floor of the four-storey restaurant building. The ground floor was the restaurant, the second floor the kitchen, the third floor was the butchers and the fourth floor was me. My room was the size of the average living room and had no windows except for a skylight. I had squeezed in a bed, table and chairs, drawers, some shelving, my record player and video set-up and crammed it full of merchandise.

It wasn't exactly legal, it wasn't even registered for habitation, and it wasn't particularly safe, but what the building inspectors didn't see didn't hurt them.

"One day it will be many bedsits, when work is done, but not yet," Mr Chandra said when we agreed to the deal. "If you caught, you squatting, OK? And no smoking! You smoke and fall asleep, whole building burn down. Deathtrap!"

I wasn't sure about his salesmanship, but I took his point.

I paid him what I could afford when I could afford it and he seemed happy with that.

Most important for me, I could park the van safely in the yard, which was fully enclosed within the building and there was always someone around twenty-four seven to keep an eye on it; people preparing, delivering and receiving food.

All I cared about was that the bedsit was perfect for my needs. I was bang in the centre of town, safe and secure, and I could more or less do what I wanted.

< < < <   > > > >

"You need to see this," Bal said as soon as I walked into the house.

"See what?" I said. Instead of explaining, he was heading up the stairs and waving for me to follow him.

"Bal," I said, "don't tell me you've got a new puppy."

"Come on!" he said.

He sounded serious.

I followed him.

Bal was one of the original lads from junior school who I'd banded together with from day one. He was the oldest of five brothers and sisters and the first of his family to be born in the UK. As such, he had the challenge of growing up simultaneously in both Asian and Western cultures. Whereas a lot of kids I knew coped by leading double-lives, Bal dealt with it by making his own decisions and standing his ground on both sides of the fence. This meant a life of constant conflict; at home, at school, and more or less everywhere he went.

"Everyone's telling me what to do," he would say, "and I can't please all of them, so I may as well please myself and do what I want to do."

For years he would have massive arguments with his dad, but if anyone bad-mouthed his family, then he'd be fighting with them, too.

As I got older, I appreciated more and more how brave he was to stand up to everyone around him, day after day. And it wasn't that he didn't get knocked down; he did, repeatedly.

He and his dad called a truce when he left school and during the holidays from studying his A-Levels, Bal worked in his dad's textile factory in Foleshill.

When ever I asked Bal when he was going to take over the family business, his answer was always 'never'.

"I'm not going to see the world by staring at sewing machines all day, am I?"

He spoke about joining the army, which made sense to me as someone who'd seen his share of conflict, plus it had the added bonus of doing something completely opposed to his father's aspirations.

For as long as I had known them, the family had lived in a sprawling three-storey corner terraced house on Foleshill Road, near the Saracen's Head. It was three times the size of the neighbouring properties, with huge sash-windows and a labyrinth of corridors, staircases and rooms, six different fire places and two kitchens. There was also a newsagent which opened onto the corner, but I was never quite sure whether the family owned it or not. The house was always a hive of constant activity, it was more like a community-centre. There were the five kids and all their mates congregating there, three generations of the extended family visiting, cooking was a non-stop activity, business deals were discussed in sitting rooms, there was always a birthday, anniversary or a celebration being either planned or actually taking place.

It had been the scene where I'd witnessed family arguments and the grandest and greatest parties of all my childhood.

At the end of a corridor on the third floor in one of the smallest bedrooms, Bal's younger brother Barrath and two of his mates hunched over computer keyboards, their faces illuminated by the green writing on their screens.

"Hey Barrath," I said. He was fifteen and had none of Bal's fierce independence, whereas Bal was always out doing stuff, Barrath was usually inside 'working on something'.

I gathered Bal wanted to show me what these kids were doing on the computers, but I didn't imagine it would interest me in the slightest. Computers were for libraries and launching rockets as far as I knew.

"They've written a game," Bal said and nudged Barrath, who looked around for some kind of approval from me.

I shrugged as if to say, 'Go on then', but computer games weren't my thing. Fiddling with a joystick to play Space Invaders, Pacman and Asteroids didn't interest me. I'd rather put ten pence in a fruit machine.

Barrath explained, "We've hacked the Dungeon Master game and recoded it to be about fighting football fans. It's called 'Casuals Massacre'."

"Barrath mate," I said, "I think I understood about three words of that."

He nodded sympathetically, and said, "Just watch."

He turned back to the computer and the blank screen was replaced by a blocky picture of a footie-casual and the game logo.

"Casuals Massacre," I said. "It's got a ring to it, but what is it?"

"It's a game. You go through these tunnels and fight the monsters and Villa fans."

"And kill them!" Barrath's mate said.

I laughed and patted him on the back, "I like it so far."

We all watched the screen like moths staring at fireworks as Barrath continued with the demonstration. There were dark dungeon corridors that he moved down and junctions where he had to decide which way to go and eventually he'd meet some bad-guys and have to kill them. The screen would flash like a strobe light as the fighting kicked off and then Barrath's hands were going ten-to-the-dozen on the keyboard as his mates cheered him on to victory, which was all great. I had no idea that computers could create pictures like that, but it just wasn't for me.

"It's grand lads," I said, "very impressive, but I don't have a computer and I'm not looking to buy computer games."

"We don't want you to buy it," Barrath said. He looked at his mates for final approval, then looked up at me and said, "We want you to sell it."

<<<< >>>>

I spent the rest of Sunday afternoon with my mum in Bedworth.

Derek, her boyfriend of a few years, had said the locals pronounce it like the sound of a brick landing in a canal 'b-duff'. They'd bought the house together after deciding to move in together. Mum said there was no way she was moving into 'another woman's house' meaning Derek's old house and they soon found and fell in love with their 'new house'. She'd talk all the time about the high-ceilings and the 'massive' garden, which needed some work, but they were determined to 'make it nice' together.

I was happy for her.

I always knocked, although mum had told me not to. She answered the door in her 'Sunday jumper' which was a cream-coloured oversized knitwear thing she'd had for years.

I took her a pirate copy of Top Gun on VHS, a bottle of wine and two pairs of Levi's each for her and Derek, even though I'd never seen him wear jeans, ever.

"Look at you," she said and we hugged. "How've you been?"

"I've been good, mum," I smiled. "What about you?"

"I'm good," she said, "Business is good, I have a new client and some new staff which is always fun." She was an animated talker, and her long ponytail whipped around her shoulders as she spoke.

My mum is the Queen of the Ponytail. I must've seen her produce it a million times; with four strokes of her hairbrush she'd gather her hair together at the back and then magically transfer a hair-band to the back of her head. And there it would be; a thick plume of long brown hair that would swish and sway in her wake. It's always been her default hairstyle when she's at home or working or shopping or any other time she means business. Only at parties or on nights out would she let her hair down. But, even then, if anything happened that called for action, a spilt drink or a dropped plate, like Wonder Woman, she'd retrieve her hair band and with a flourish there'd be her ponytail and whatever the problem was would be dealt with.

And she wasn't afraid to take control. She didn't deliberate and she didn't dip her toe to test the water, she dived in with both feet and people would either applaud or stare in silent awe.

"Help me or get out of my way," she'd said to her cleaning colleagues at work.

She said the same thing to a nosey rambler when I was six and broke my collarbone by rolling down Corley Rocks. We had no car and there wasn't a phone for miles. "Help me or get out of my way!"

And she used to say it in the kitchen about ten times a day. "Steve, if you're not going to help, get out of my way."

Failure to comply would result in a hefty shove, a wet cloth in the face, or a hot baking tray singeing your arm hairs.

People learned quickly around my mum.

"Where'd these come from?" she asked, studying the jeans.

"Back of a lorry, literally," I said. "Don Andrews."

About three weeks before Christmas, late on Sunday night, I had a phone call from Don, who had a job for me.

Don was a 24 Hour Recovery Driver, which meant that the police would call him out to recover crashed vehicles.

I don't know how much he got paid for this, but it had one perk that was fairly profitable for him, and for me, hence the reason for the late-night call.

Don owned an enormous tow-truck and basically, when the police got called out to an accident involving a lorry or a van, they would call Don to drag it out of a ditch and deliver it to a recovery yard. However, knowing that the contents of the vehicle would disappear at some point, they decided it might as well disappear sooner rather than later. Which is where I would come in.

Once the driver had been taken to the hospital or wherever he was going, the police would call Don and they'd assess the contents. The police had first dibs. They'd fill their squad cars with whatever they fancied and then me and Don would take what was left. I didn't want to know whatever deal Don did with the police, but I'd split my profits with Don fifty-fifty.

The officers would then take some photos showing how the lorry had been mercilessly ransacked, and they'd leave.

This would happen once every few months or so, and Don, an old friend of dad's, had been doing it for years. My arrangement with him had been going a few months and occasionally came up trumps, and sometimes not. A particular favourite was a van full of David Bowie tour T-shirts which I sold as exclusive merchandise before even the first concert of the tour.

This night was better. I'd left the scene of the accident with the back of the van piled high with brand new Levi's jeans in every size available. 501s, shrink-to-fit, stretch-fit, Stay Prest, orange tab, red-lined, every style in blue, black, grey, red. You name it; I had it.

As soon as I was back at the bedsit, I made sure there was a small selection of the loot left for Mr Chandra, call it a month's rent.

"I don't want you involved in anything that's not legit," mum said.

"It was a Don Andrews job," I said. "All above board."

She knew Don, which meant she wasn't one-hundred percent convinced on the 'above board' claim, but accepted the gifts.

When I offered to help her with the cooking, Mum had me stirring the gravy. I was sure that this was a wind-up, and it didn't need stirring for like twenty minutes (if so, there's a massive market opportunity there). My mum had a wicked sense of humour, verging on cruel. When I was a kid, every Sunday, my mum asked my dad to peal a bowl full of grapes for the fruit salad. It went on for weeks, and he dutifully did as she asked. Eventually, he caught her laughing, and she took pleasure in confessing she had been winding him up, but it was only a matter of time before she'd have him again.

A benefit of helping in the kitchen was avoiding spending an uncomfortable hour with Derek watching Ski Sunday.

He was a decent bloke, and he'd always been great to mum, but I kept my distance. Not that I had a problem with him or anything, but family-scenes like Sunday dinner were a strain for me. It was just too weird and awkward.

Derek was forty-something, had broad shoulders and stood six-foot tall. He was not in bad shape, except for his paunchy belly that spilled over his belt, like all the fat in his body had congregated in the one place. His thick military-crop of brown hair had flecks of grey. He had a long-reaching neck and a prominent Adam's apple that pushed out as he spoke. His teeth were a little long and looked longer in his narrow mouth, which he's inadvisably decorated with the heavy moustache. When he spoke, this narrow collection of features somehow got even narrower. He also wore really strong aftershave all the time.

He didn't seem to own a pair of jeans and wore only trousers from a suit or what my dad had called 'slacks'. I'd never even seen him in a T-shirt. Even at his most relaxed at home, he wore polo shirts and brand new slippers. I guess he was big on appearance and saw his role in life to bring order to all around him, whether it was required or not. He wasn't pushy, but if someone asked him, he always had a good answer, or at least an informed opinion.

Derek divorced about ten years ago and he had a daughter, Zoe, who was 'engaged to be married', which was his favourite subject of conversation and another reason for me to hang out in the kitchen.

I think my mum expected us to bond over the fact that Derek's company was a minor sponsor of Coventry City. He got invited to lots of corporate events and to what they called the "executive club". How she expected this bonding to take place, I'm not sure, because I wasn't that impressed by 'executive status' and Derek had no interest in football, apart from the commercial benefits of being a minor sponsor to a First Division side.

We shook hands every time we met like we were reconfirming a business arrangement and that he was constantly monitoring my performance and development.

Derek had business in Bournemouth on Monday morning. Mum insisted he drove down that evening and stay in a hotel.

"It's safer," she said, "I hate to think of him getting up at the crack of dawn and driving all that way on the icy roads."

We didn't need to speak about the root of this fear, and I could see that Derek didn't want to put her through the worry.

My mum worked as a cleaner when my dad died. She'd stepped into his shoes in more ways than one. She became the main breadwinner in the family, not by default, but by starting her own cleaning company.

"I can't afford to work for other people anymore," she said. Her one-woman enterprise soon won enough clients to take on more staff and soon employed three cleaners working full-time.

She threw herself into it becoming borderline obsessive about how 'We provide the best service there is and there's no one better'.

One of her new clients was Derek's company, and she impressed him with her dedication to the task and he was obviously very 'taken' by her, as he put it.

I was in my early teens when they started 'going out' and after a few years they bought the house together and mum assumed I'd move in with them, but there was no way I was moving to Bedworth. There's nothing wrong with the place, lovely people, but it's not where I belong. I moved into the Taj Mahal bedsit, which broke mum's heart, but I was sixteen and knew my own mind.

CHAPTER THREE

Monday 12th January 1987

Coventry market was a West-Midlands bazaar, where hundreds of stalls sold anything and everything. The huge circular building, as big as a cricket pitch with a car park on the roof. Six days a week, bargain hunters crammed within its round perimeter wall. Stalls packed the entire floor space, some the size of a small house and some a trestle table. The feeding frenzy of frantic shoppers found the best stalls. The market was a carnival of people, a sea of nodding heads packed in like sardines, all of them smiling as they held out their money. Arms would wave money and grab change in the constant carnage of trade and bartering. The smell was a blend of new leather, candy floss and fish, depending on how close you were to the separate Fish Market section.

Having worked on the market for two years, I know the market like the back of my hand and I could manoeuvre through the round labyrinth of alleyways and aisles. You had to keep an eye at though, as there was always someone doing a U-turn as they realised they were lost which was easily done inside a round hall of that size.

Molly sold clothes, menswear, the gear you'd want to go out in on a Saturday night.

She wore low-cut tops, peroxide-hair, figure-hugging spray-on designer jeans and the permanent six-inch stilettos. Her hair was as white as milk and as wild as a sheep's fleece, but the first thing you'd notice about her was her signature blusher. It was a splash of blood-red on her cheeks, a startling colour that always sent a chill down my spine and a naughty glow in my belly.

She beamed a smile the second she saw me making my way through the crowd with an army kit-bag on my shoulder. Molly would track crowd movement like a hawk, seeing everything. No one could slip under her radar.

She was a former-work acquaintance of my dad and an old friend of my mum's. When I left school, I worked on her stall. She showed me the ropes of market trading and enhanced my general life-skills. Like most people, that first year after leaving school my life changed so much it was the best and the worst time of my life. I developed a thick skin, learned a lot about reading people and always being on the front foot. Molly was a Jedi-master at these things and an excellent teacher.

She would teach me by mantras, such as, 'I don't mind bullshitters, but I can't stand liars'.

Suffice to say, she's a spicy character who could hold her own in the hustle and bustle of running her stall.

With selling, she understood the power of presentation too. 'Put your best strawberries on top, Stevie,' as she'd told me many times.

"Hello sailor," she said, hoisting up the hinged bar-door for me to board her raised command-post.

I dropped the bag to give her a hug and a kiss on that blood-red cheek. I breathed in the pleasant scent of Chanel no5.

"How've you been?" she said.

"I've been good," I said, "very good, thanks. What about you? What you been up to?"

"Work hard, play hard," she smiled. "You know me."

Shirley, the Saturday-girl who worked six days a week, was leant over the counter reading a glossy magazine.

"Hi Steve," she said, looking up with a warm smile.

She wore a black leather jacket and a vinyl mini-skirt so tight it looked cling film on a pork roast. Shirley was a mini-Molly, but they weren't related, as far as I knew.

"Shirley," I said. "What's happening?"

"Busy, busy," she said and dropped me a wink.

Molly snatched the magazine from the counter before Shirley even blinked. "Busy are ya? I'm thinking we might need a full stock-check, then you'll be really busy."

Shirley smiled and straightened up.

Molly turned back to me. "How's your mum?"

"She's great. I was there for Sunday dinner yesterday," I said.

"Are you courtin' then or what?" she asked, pointing the question at me like a sharp prod in the ribs.

I hesitated before answering, just for a split-second, but it was more than enough. "No-"

Molly's forefinger, with its manicured fingernail, jumped up to silence me. "Come on, tell me! Who is she?"

"There's no one," I said, but I knew it was hopeless.

"You can't lie to me, young man," she scorned.

I tried to weather this storm, but then came the clincher: "I held you as a baby!"

I didn't know what that meant and was too scared to ask.

A customer saved me. He was a wanna-be football casual looking for a 'decent jumper' even though in terms of terrace fashion he was three years too late.

"Pringle or Lacoste?" Molly asked him.

"Lyle and Scott?" he said.

"What do you want that for?" she said, shaking her head. "No one wants Lyle and Scott anymore."

The lad flushed red with embarrassment and his shoulders visibly deflated.

"Is it real then, your stuff?" he asked. "I don't wanna buy anything fake."

Molly leaned over the counter and pushed her chest out. "Of course my stock's real you cheeky git," she told him, "but your balls won't be if you carry on with the lip."

Realising that he was seriously outgunned, he made his purchase and left with a red V-neck Pringle, a bargain at thirty quid and a very nice choice if you're into that kind of thing.

"Well," Molly said to me, "I suppose you want a cup of tea and I doubt if that bag's got your laundry in. Is this a business or personal visit?"

"A bit of both, as always," I told her.

Shirley took over the stall, I grabbed the navy bag, and we retired to the small, private space behind the backboard for a cup of tea and a chin wag.

The first item on the agenda was my failure to deny the 'courtin' question and I gave up the minimal amount of information that I could.

"She's alright, really good-looking, dead-posh, but not stuck up," I summarised.

Molly nodded and smiled, "Little rich girl, eh? Where does she buy her clothes?"

"Nowhere round here," I said. "She's like something out of 'Pretty in Pink' or something. More Hollywood Boulevard than Holyhead Road."

"How many times have you seen her?"

"None yet," I sighed, "not really."

"Well, when you do get together with her, Stevie, she'll fall head over heels," she said. "You mark my words. A girl like her will have never seen the likes of you before. You're irresistible, even on a bad day."

I left thirty minutes later without the bag and with a deal for half of the profits from the Levis.

"It's good stuff, but it's gonna take a while to move it," Molly had said. "Do you want anything upfront?"

I shook my head, "No need."

"Tell your mum I'll see her down the Bull and Anchor on Friday night, yeah?"

"I will," I said, "And take care of yourself."

I had one more stop in the market before moving on and that was to a stall that I'd never frequented before.

'Computers and Games' was a new enterprise and hopefully keen to establish themselves.

I had one of Barrath's games in my pocket and a business proposition to put to them.

< < < <   > > > >

The art of copying VHS videos was partly down to skill and partly down to hardware. I had developed the skill and bought the hardware; two high-end video recorders with tracking capability, and although it was unavoidable that the copy would degrade, the results I could achieve were pretty good.

I didn't want to get into the pirate movies market as it was fast moving, drew too much unwanted attention and there were too many loose lips sinking too many ships.

So, as I say, I didn't particularly want to be in a customer-facing role. Instead, I set myself up as a wholesaler. I could provide quality products and charge a premium, which I did. I'm sure most of my customers assumed the tapes were originals with the labelling removed to prevent trace-ability, but of course, they were all my own handiwork from the two machines in my bedsit.

I'd come up with the idea of being a provider with a guy named Barney Rubble, aka Bernard Hubble, who was the storeman at Motor Cabs, a factory next to Dunlop in Holbrooks.

(I knew Barney through his son, who also worked there and was, of course, known as Bam Bam).

"Blue movies," Barney explained. "There's market for it, I just need the tapes."

I wasn't a big fan to be honest, but business is business. Chris provided me with a library of films to copy and I started making copies. I took out my marker pen and labelled each as a first division team. Liverpool, Arsenal, West Brom.

The blokes at Barney's work loved it and would knowing ask 'Have you seen Ipswich?' and 'Southampton wasn't bad'.

Barney would rent out the tapes to his blue-collar colleagues under the guise of them visiting his locked stores to collect some safety gloves, a new handle for a file or whatever. They turned up at his storeroom (where, for security, he was the only one allowed to enter) and they collected a video.

Whether or not this was a genius marketing strategy, I kept my distance using Barney as the buffer. I just supplied the tapes to Barney and what he did with them was his business. Like I said to him, you pay your money, you take your chances.

Things were going well by all accounts, few customers complained, although how could they?

I advised him when he started this venture; find the optimum number of customers and don't go beyond that or someone's going to say something to someone and you'll end up getting caught.

Barney had been in touch and wanted more movies. Hence, I had another twenty videos in a carrier bag.

We'd arranged to meet in a batch bar called Alfie's on the train bridge where Holbrooks Lane became Lockhurst Lane.

I was already a connoisseur of Coventry's batch bars and my speciality was gauging whether the sincerity of the person serving equated to the quality of the food and drink they provided. There were exceptions, but I found that people happy in their work delivered a higher quality product.

New establishments were hard to judge because the staff were often the business-owners and very keen to make a go of things, but Alfie's was at the other end of the scale; in terms of the business's life-cycle, Alfie's should have been retired to a knackers yard years ago. This was my fourth visit to the establishment, all regarding dealings with Barney, and I found the service and quality consistently abysmal. Either to cut costs or because no one wanted to work with him, Alfie's was a one-man band. Alfie took your order when you went in, took your money, made your order up whilst you took a seat and shouted you to come get it when he'd plated it up. He was also a miserable bastard and smoked enough to leave a brown stain on the ceiling above the cooker.

As usual, there was no one in the queue at the counter.

White tiles lined the four walls, most of which had miraculously survived the blitz. Two oddly selected reproduced paintings of young children with dogs completed the establishments' interior decoration.

There were two other patrons at separate tables, both reading the Racing Post, but neither seemed to want to discuss their shared sporting interest with the other.

The carpet was well-trodden, possibly once green, and much the same feel as a concrete floor.

Alfie looked up from his cigarette as I walked in. Mild annoyance that was actually a slight improvement animated his miserable face.

"Two teas and two bacon and egg batches, please," I said.

"Two pound twenty," he said and took a step forward to collect my cash.

I paid the man and took a seat in the corner.

From where I sat, I could see some activity around the gates of Motor Cabs main entrance, which meant it was dinner time for the few hundred staff and that Barney would be along any minute. I'd sometimes see lorries piled high with the metal frames of lorry cabs on the trailer, so I guessed that's what they made.

Not that it mattered to me.

What did matter to me, and what mattered to Barney, was that he wanted more films. And, even more importantly, I had new films in a Co-op carrier bag topped with lettuce leaves to act as a cunning disguise for Barney to slip the items back into the factory. (Although almost all the security staff were regular customers, so I didn't think he'd have a problem somehow).

Barney was ten minutes late. He only had thirty minutes dinner-break, and he looked stressed when he came in. The bacon batch I'd bought him was cold and the tea was going the same way. Barney sat down without a word of thanks. Don't worry about it, I thought, my shout. And I remembered I didn't particularly like Barney.

"I need more tapes," he said. "Did you get some?". He snatched up the batch and devoured it.

"What do you want more tapes for?" I said.

"More tapes mean more money," he said. The batch was almost gone and he was starting on the tea. "I can double my takings," he said, "maybe more than double, who knows? Easy."

I shook my head. "Supply and demand only applies to an open market," I explained. "What you have is a closed market. It's limited to the employees of the factory. You need to be very careful and selective when you think about expanding your client-base. If you ask me, Barney, stay exclusive. You can keep making a tidy profit and stay beneath the radar. The more people you involve in this enterprise, the more you risk someone's gonna say the wrong thing to the wrong person and that'll be the end of the movie business for you because you'll be getting the arse.".

"Did you bring more tapes or not?" he said, scoffing the last mouthful of his batch.

"Barney, are you listening to me?"

He wasn't.

"How many you got?"

"All together? Right now?"

He nodded at each question.

"Twenty," I said.

"I'll take them."

"They're five pounds each," I told him.

"One hundred pounds?" he asked.

I nodded.

It's at this point that he stops to think for the first time in our conversation.

But the pause is brief.

He reached for his wallet and pulled out five twenty-pound notes.

I snatched the money from his hand and I snapped at him, "What are you doing!"

Something in their papers still engrossed the two Racing Post guys, but more workers were wandering in. Nobody was looking. "You need to be careful," I told him.

He still wasn't listening.

I'm thinking it's time to re-evaluate our business arrangement, but then the risk to me is small to non-existent.

"Where are the films?" he asks.

I push the shopping bag across the floor with my foot.

"Enjoy," I say.

I get up and leave.

After marvelling again at how huge Sarah's house was, I almost left the clipboard in the van and bottled the whole questionnaire-thing, but I knew that a conventional approach was not going to fly with this girl, who must get pickup lines multiple-times a day. So I had to stand out from the crowd.

People who say 'just be yourself' never get anywhere. The problem with 'just being yourself' is that everyone else is doing the same and they're nothing more than a face in the crowd. But if I could make her laugh, she'd be at least listening to what I said next.

So I grabbed my Parker pen and my clipboard with the typed-out questions numbered one to five and strode up the driveway to meet my destiny.

I rang the bell and timed my smile to coincide perfectly with the opening of the door, but instead of Sarah, I was greeted by a man who I assumed was her father.

And he wasn't smiling.

His silk shirt bridged his chest and everything below tapered down to his feet. He was built like an athlete and had a thick Mexican-bandit moustache.

Before I could say anything, he stepped back, grabbed the videos, and held them out for me.

"Thank you," he said, in a dismissive gesture.

"Did you enjoy them?" I asked him, juggling the clipboard and pen to buy some time, although his frown was telling me he wasn't selling any.

"I didn't watch them," he said, and again offered the videos for me to take. It was like a gut-punch. My hands stayed at my side, to his growing annoyance.

He raised the videos as if he was about to throw them to me.

I took the one off the top of the stack and tucked it under my arm. As I took the second one, I raised my voice to ask, "You didn't watch them? I hope you didn't waste your money."

"My daughter said they were free!" he snapped. "It's too late to ask me for money now."

"No, no. They are free," I said. "I just wanted to know if you enjoyed the films."

And then I heard her voice. "Is that the 'mobil' video guy?" she asked as she skipped down the stairs.

"Hi," I said, taking the third and final video from her father.

He rolled his eyes and said, "He was just leaving."

"Oh?" Sarah said. She appeared at his side and tilted her head to the left. "I thought you wanted my feedback?"

"I do, if that's OK?" I smiled and raised the trusty clipboard, "It will only take five minutes of your time but will be invaluable to me and my business."

She'd tied her hair up with a scrunchie and beneath her baggy denim jacket, she wore a blue t-shirt with the Superman logo across her chest. She had red football socks pulled up over grey screen-wash jeans and open laced blue boxing shoes.

Nobody I know dresses like this, I told myself.

The hallway had no ceiling and rose to a skylight. At its centre was a spiral staircase that curved away from the wall at the bottom to meet another at the top. There were more doors than I'd ever seen in a single house, and Sarah led me to the one opposite.

The door led to a spacious kitchen.

"Please take a seat," she said, waving at the chairs around a dark wood kitchen table, which was big enough for snooker.

I sat.

The kitchen was an expanse of space that at first seemed unnecessary, but then it all seemed to be useful. There was a huge length of kitchen top that looked like, and probably were, a single piece of granite. The cupboards were a dark brown wood that matched the kitchen table. Apart from two ovens and a fridge the size of a garage door, a soda-stream and a microwave oven, there weren't any other visible appliances, unless they were built into the dark wood cupboards.

Why did they have two ovens? Where was the washing machine?

She hauled open one of the heavy fridge doors. The shelves of the door held every kind of chilled drink that I could imagine.

"Coke?" she asked, taking a can from one of the many that stood beside the orange juice in a milk bottle.

I nodded, "Thanks."

"Or Pepsi?" she added.

"Pepsi," I said, relying on instinct, as it sounded more sophisticated.

She chose Pepsi too, but I wasn't sure if this was a conscious decision or an act of solidarity with me.

"I have some admin questions first, if that's OK?" I said as she sat across the table.

I opened my Pepsi, dropped the ring pull in the can, and took a sip.

"Oh my God!" she said. "You just put your ring pull in the can."

I nodded.

"I've never seen anyone do that," she said.

"Well, stick around," I grinned, "I'm full of surprises."

She smiled.

"You've really never seen that before?"

She shook her head. "You're my first weirdo!"

"Oh," I said, "Cool."

"Alright. Fire away," she said, nodding at the clipboard.

"Name?"

"Sarah Morales."

"OK, that's the admin out of the way. Question One, what is your favourite movie of all time?"

"E.T." she said without hesitation.

"Really?" I wrote it down. "You don't want more time to think about?"

"No, not at all," she smiled. "Don't you like it?"

"I love it," I said. "It's in my top ten, but I thought you'd be more Breakfast Club or Dangerous Liaisons."

"Angsty-teen is not my thing," she sighed, "and I don't go for romance."

"That's a pity," I said.

Her expressionless gaze cracked into a smile.

One-nil to me.

We both laughed. It was fun.

"Next question?" she asked.

I consulted my clipboard. "Question 2. Did you rewind the films after watching?"

"Yes," she nodded, then paused, "maybe, I'm not sure. Yes. I remember."

"Are you certain?" I said, reaching for the three videos, "I don't want to put a tick on my sheet and then have to turn it into a cross."

"I'm saying 'Yes'," she said, taking a long swig of Pepsi. "If not, sue me."

"I'll take your word for it," I said, and ticked the box for Yes. "Question Three. Do you prefer red or brown sauce?"

She shook her head. "I don't need to make the choice. I've solved the conundrum."

I was thrilled that she had entered the spirit of my little game, and every word she said multiplied my intrigue.

"And how do you think you've done that?" I asked, "One of the biggest quandaries of our generation, debated by philosophers around the planet without resolution, and yet you've solved it?"

"Yep," she said.

I raised my eyebrows and gestured for her to spill the beans.

"I have both," she said. "On the same plate. I just pour them both on. All over."

I faked a stutter.

She laughed.

"Oh my God," I gasped. "You've solved the eternal problem. We should publish a paper. The Oxford Press will be drooling over this."

"Do you want to be my agent?"

"I could be," I nod. "My rates are very competitive."

"I bet they are," she smiled.

I looked up. She had a pre-giggle expression. She was fantastic-looking and the greatest fun to be with.

"I solved the chicken and egg thing too," she said. "Chickens come from dinosaurs, who come from eggs, so the very first chicken came from an egg. Therefore, egg before chicken."

"Goddam! That was my next question," I said and crossed out Question Four.

"You're so stupid," she said. "What's it got to do with movies, anyway?"

I looked back at my clipboard and pretended to write something.

I was there, Question Five, written on the page, 'Will you go out with me?'.

This was my plan, to create a perfect moment, to make her laugh and then ask her out, simple as that.

Just ask her, I told myself.

And she was laughing. Smiling so much when she tried to sip her Pepsi, she had to stop.

"Last question?" she said. "I hope it's a good one."

I looked up from the clipboard, aware that my expression was one of grinning stupidity.

"Question Five," I said, "is...

CHAPTER FOUR

Saturday 24th January 1987

The next few weeks were a torturous inverse of the world that I thought I lived in. My life was reversed, like a photographic negative. I found comfort in misery and felt guilty when I found humour in anything. All I could think of was Sarah. I thought I saw her everywhere, but every time I was wrong. I analysed every word we'd said, going over and over what I could remember of our conversation. I dreaded that I would never see her again and, in the darkest times, when it hurt the most, I almost wished I hadn't met her at all.

But then I stopped myself wallowing in self-pity and tried to snap out of it.

I just wanted to see her. I wanted to hear her voice, to be in the same room as her. To be with her.

And I regretted not seeing my Questionnaire Plan through to the end.

I'd bottled it.

I'd sat there and saw the words on the page - Will you go out with me?

Then I'd looked up at Sarah and said, "...will you be renting from Movies To You in the future?"

She held her smile to disguise her disappointment, although it was nothing compared to mine. "Will I have to pay next time?" she'd asked as laughter burst from her lips.

And so I had to wait until Saturday night for a legitimate excuse to go back to Riverdale Close.

I thought about just showing up, knocking on her door, opening my heart and spilling my guts. I thought about these things every minute of every day, but I didn't act on them. I didn't want to seem desperate, but I was.

Finally, Saturday night rolled around. I dropped Andy off and headed back to Riverdale Close and knocked on that door again.

But nobody was home.

I was heartbroken.

I hung around in the van for thirty minutes, then left.

<<<< >>>>

Even a history-making event on Sunday, watching City live on TV for the first time, didn't raise my spirits. We drew nil-nil away to Arsenal which was a commendable result against title contenders.

On Monday morning I stayed in recording bootleg tapes, trimming the printed cardboard cassette in-fills, folding them into the plastic holder and writing the title and band on the tape's label.

Metallica. Sheffield City Hall. September 18 1986.

Bruce Springsteen. Newcastle United FC. June 5th 1986.

U2. NEC Arena Birmingham. November 12th 1984.

I kept the writing neat and tidy. It felt good to focus my mind on a simple, repetitive task. I had over two hundred tape boxes ready by mid-afternoon and twenty tapes recorded and ready to go. The rest I would stock up by demand.

I think the music industry has always been one where the line between what's legal and what's not is constantly evolving and always blurry. When John Lennon and Paul McCartney started making music, they didn't even know that a song could be owned, and they wrote a couple of decent tunes. Live music, especially, is sent out into the air for anyone within listening distance to enjoy. And some of those people capture the sound and come away with a recording of it. Other people, in turn, become potential customers for such a recording, which therefore creates a market, that the music industry has no intention of fulfilling. And that creates a market opportunity. They could put out live albums every week, but they choose not to.

It should be remembered that music fans are the lifeblood of the recording industry. These are the people that buy records and attend concerts. So why the industry chooses to starve their desires and shun their profits is beyond me.

Don Andrews, my vehicle recovery friend, was one of these music consumers. For Don, the catalogue of music that a band had officially released was insufficient. He wanted more. And he had acquired more of the music he loved by purchasing what is commonly referred to as 'bootleg' albums which are available on the black market and marginally illegal in most cases, according to the previously mentioned blurry/moving line.

For years Don had travelled the country to Record Fairs and regularly purchased such LPs. He had a network of contacts that could source desired items from the States or Europe and even Japan.

Don had his finger on the pulse of the music industry and, more importantly, over two-hundred bootleg LPs.

"The Rolling Stones 1978, Some Girls 'Live in Texas'," he would tell me, holding up his coveted record. "Better than anything they've released, as a live show, it's close to perfect rock'n'roll and the sound quality is amazing."

I didn't doubt it, but I've never listened to it, although I'd sold over twenty copies of it.

In partnership with Don, I'd seen an opportunity and set about doing a little market research in order to find similar people who were happy to part with a small fee in return for a cassette-copy of these sought-after bootlegs. I found these people by placing personal ads in the music papers like Sounds, NME, Melody Maker, asking if they are fans of listening to live music and an invitation to respond to a PO Box. If they did so, then I would reply with a list of live bootleg recordings that I could supply them on a C90 cassette at £2 a throw payable by cheque or postal order.

The buyer then posted orders to Flat no 2, Taj Mahal, Longfriars Street, Coventry, and I sent them the requested tape. In a good week I'd be at the Post Office to cash in thirty or forty quid in postal orders.

< < < <   > > > >

Somehow I got through the week to the next Saturday and we had West Ham at home.

It was getting to the end of January and it was freezing. I pulled the cuffs of my ski-jacket down over my hands and made my way into town. I met the lads for a full-English in Fishy Moore's.

Chris was telling us that The Parson's Nose, a preferred chippie of mine, had been busted for serving a customer an actual rat that had fallen into the fryer and dished up as a battered fish.

We've learnt to take what Chris tells us with a pinch of salt. It's not worth pulling him up on every occasion. But you couldn't help but to like Chris.

I can still picture him on our first ever day in junior school; my mum walked me to the classroom door, handed me over to the authorities and assured me that everything would be fine.

I definitely did not feel fine.

I was told to take off my coat and hand-over my lunch bag and I did as I was told, but for some reason even I was less fine without my coat. Then I walked into the class-room and saw Chris. There were ten other kids there too, but I only remember him.

He was grinning. He seemed to know something no one else did. I wanted to know what it was. I wanted to smile like that, too. He made me forget that I didn't feel fine and that my mum had abandoned me to this strange place and people I didn't know.

Of course, there was nothing funny. Nothing in particular, anyway. Chris just wore a permanent grin, it was his default expression and it still is. It's got him in trouble a few times over the years, and it's led to a lot of fun too.

His other dominant trait, which didn't complement his perma-grin, was his lack of academic prowess. Words weren't a particularly strong point and when they weren't forth-coming, he'd accentuate the grin to fill in the waiting time for his brain to catch up. Chris has the attention span of a goldfish on speed and the mental agility of a spanner and whilst his brain worked through a problem, his body would wander off and do whatever it pleased.

Throughout our school-lives we had enjoyed a shared pursuit of mischief.

Our towering achievement occurred, at the end of a long wintry school day in a forlorn senior school chemistry class, me and Chris, using the available apparatus, flooded the Science block over night. We filled a class-room sink with an inch of water and attached a small length of hose to a tap. Then we took the over-flow plug, the thing that looked like a plastic dick, and packed it with wet paper towels. Before leaving for the day, we turned the tap onto a slow drip. Anyone passing the sink would see it contained water but was essentially harmless.

And it worked. The next day, the sink had overflowed and flooded the science block. It had then frozen solid.

This was not my finest hour. But in my defence, which I appreciate is not the most robust, we only did it for a laugh, which I admit doesn't sound great no matter how you say it. Not that it would elicit a confession from us. They'd never take us alive!

The following day, as all classes were cancelled and the school assessed the devastation, the entire class was lined-up and we were told that as the culprit was in this room, no one was going to leave until those responsible came forward. The matter was to be handed over to the police as the damages incurred were many thousands of pounds and may result in prosecution.

Chris stood there grinning. They marched him to the front for interrogation, but he didn't crack. He just kept smiling and they eventually released him as a suspect, saying he was 'too stupid' to come up with such an elaborate scheme.

The perpetrators were never caught.

Where Chris did excel at school in a positive way was gymnastics, mainly because he knew no fear and when attempting a physical feat of any kind, he would never consider the potential for injury.

Even at junior school, he could walk on his hands, and he often did. It was a legitimate alternative form of travel to Chris and instructions not to do so either didn't register or were cast into the backseat of his mind and forgotten. In gym class he would tight-rope walk on top of the climbing apparatus. The swings in the park became his parallel bars for his enjoyment and our entertainment.

He would take a running jump from the top board at Cov baths with the aim of 'reaching the other side of the pool'. How he expected to perform a landing on the tiled floor from a fifty-foot fall was never clear, but he came close a few times.

The danger he faced in the gymnastics arena was tame in comparison and one high-ranking trainer singled him out as a protege in the sport. A potential Olympic career never materialised, however, due to 'disciplinary issues' after not turning up for many prestigious events.

Chris laughed it off like he laughed off most things. He was fun and he was funny. And he got funnier as we went through school, sometimes intentionally, sometimes not.

On one occasion, after being the first to solve a conundrum that was eluding the rest of us, Chris proudly proclaimed that 'I'm thicker than I look, you know'.

Nobody argued.

"He's as sharp as a marble," as one teacher has said.

Chris kept grinning.

< < < <   > > > >

Fishy Moore's was a proper fish bar and had been in Coventry for as long as anyone could remember. Chris reckoned it was the oldest fish and chip shop in England, and who were we to argue? He also said the woman who took you to your table was the original 'Mrs Moore', and she certainly looked old enough.

There was grease in the air, in the walls and on the tables. You could smell it everywhere and almost taste it. The smell reminded me of Friday evenings as a kid, Crackerjack, Newsround and fish and chips wrapped in newspaper. For most of the morning, the restaurant tables were quiet, the clientele mostly subdued and pensive men passing time staring at passers-by. By late afternoon the place would be packed, noisy, choc-a-block with families of kids from the swimming baths with wet hair and ferocious appetites.

We made our way to the table as Chris elaborated on the rat-tale. Behind his back, we rolled our eyes and smiled.

Chatting to the lads helped take my mind off my prospective romantic aspirations, but it did little for my peace of mind.

"By the way, I've got 501s in all your sizes," I told them, "three quid each, mates rates. How many do you want?"

"Two," Andy said.

"Two," said Bal.

"Two, one in black," Chris told me.

"Done," I said.

"Have you got red?" Chris asked.

I nodded.

"Make it three then."

We sat at the table and immediately Andy leant forward. "Have you heard? We've sold Micky Adams to Leeds!" Andy said.

"No!" I said. "Not Micky Adams?"

I had a soft-spot for Adams, he was 'a good honest player' as my dad would have said, but these were the perils of supporting a football team. Any day your favourite player could leave the club. You could be cheering an idol one week and then he's score against you the next. Mick Ferguson, Ian Wallace, Steve Hunt, Mark Hateley, Gary Gillespie, Stuart Pearce were all much-loved heroes who had all moved on. Even Terry Gibson, who scored the most famous Coventry City hat-trick of all time when we beat Liverpool 4-0 in 1983, was now at Manchester United and would be lining-up against us in the FA Cup.

Bal handed me a sports bag with some hefty contents. "A present from Barrath," he said, "there's two hundred computer games in there."

I took the bag and put it on the floor at my feet. "And he's happy with the deal, yeah?" I asked, "He gets thirty pence a game, that's sixty-quid if they all sell."

"Yeah, he's happy with that, mate. He said it took forever to do the labels. They had to do it on a type-writer and then did tags with a marker pen."

I took one disk from the bag. The game they call Critter Cull. The 'artwork' was impressive, a doodle of a raving monster with the name above it. I guessed these were what Bal called 'Tags'.

"It looks good," I said. "I'll get something to do it quicker, buy a printer or something, but the personal touch looks good."

Bal nodded. "So you want some more?"

"Let's see how these go," I said. "If they sell, I'll cast the net further afield and push the numbers up. If he can develop more games, then that would be good if the sales take off."

Recently Chris had got it into his head that the only way he was going to better himself was a life of crime, and a pause in the conversation allowed him to fill us in on his latest scheme.

He glanced to his left and right, then gestured that we should lean in to listen.

We didn't. We ate our egg and beans and black puddings and wondered what plan he'd cooked up this time.

"Dixon's," he said.

No doubt he thought that a single-word explanation was enough to fully explain this stroke of genius, but our expressions shared the same clueless declaration.

Chris stared back in apparent disbelief and waited.

"What you gonna do? Leg it out the front door with a TV under your arm?"

Chris laughed and shook his head, "No, no, no."

He ate a fork full of beans, then said, "I'm not going out the front, and I'm not legging it anywhere."

These huge clues still weren't enough to elevate us to his level of his criminality, so, reluctantly, he laid out the plan in more detail. I was happy to listen to it as long as I wasn't requested to participate, not that any of Chris's plans had ever been executed as yet.

"I've been watching the delivery vans," Chris went on, "round the back, in the yard."

We nodded and ate.

"Security is lapse," he said, stressing the word 'lapse' to emphasise the technical implications. "And lapse security," (the word had maintained its emphasis at this second reading), "is their weakest link."

We were impressed and our nodding took on a tone that demonstrated so.

"Are you gonna leg it out the back of Dixon's carrying a TV?" Bal said.

I had to smile. Bal's comic timing was the best of all of us. As Andy had said many times, 'You don't say much but when you do you still don't.' We knew what he meant.

"No," Chris said, returning the smile, pleased that we law-abiding civilians had fallen into his criminal trap. "I'm going to nick the van!"

When we asked Chris how he intended to tackle the guard, specifically, as Andy put it, 'As you're about seven stone soaking wet'.

Chris answered, "With this," and pulled a hefty cosh out of his jacket pocket. It was like a truncheon, six inches of clear plastic nylon with a heavy steel weight encased in the business end.

He tapped the table with the weighted end and we all felt it.

Bal took it off him and tapped it on his head, comically causing himself to wince.

"That is one dangerous piece of kit," he said and handed it back.

"Where did you get it?" I asked.

"Never you mind where I got it," Chris said.

"Do you know what that is?" Andy said to him in all seriousness. Before Chris could answer, he said, "That's GBH. Two years, minimum, if you used it on the street. For a security guard, I'd say it's ten years, easy."

Chris shrugged as he considered it.

"How many TVs are you nicking?" Andy laughed. "I'd say it is about a year for each TV, so good luck with that."

Chris put the cosh away. I hoped that was the last we saw of it. He was always coming up with these criminal enterprises, but nothing ever came of them. There'd be some unforeseen circumstance or finite detail that was beyond his control, forcing him to abandon his plan. In this case, ten years behind bars was another one of those finite details.

"Anyway," Chris said, moving swiftly on, "Do you want to go to Man United on Saturday?"

"No," I said.

"Why not?"

"Cos we always lose," I explained, "and it's an F.A. Cup game, so that means we'll get proper mullered."

"You said you liked going to Old Trafford," Andy said, slurping his tea.

"I do," I said, "I just don't wanna see us get battered again by a has-been club and have their has-been plastic fans taking the piss."

"We might win!" Bal countered, and we all laughed, but he looked serious.

"Anyway," I said, "Haven't we sold out our allocation, so it's all hypothetical."

"Imagine if there was no such thing as a hypothetical question," Bal said.

Chris and Andy ignored him, but I raised my finger and marked a point on the invisible scoreboard.

Bal smiled and nodded in recognition.

"I can get four tickets," Chris said.

I didn't register this at first. Subconsciously, I had been looking over their heads, scouring the room looking for...someone.

"What's up with you?" Andy said. I didn't realise he was talking to me until he punched me on the arm.

"Nothing's up with me," I said, mortally insulted by his accusation.

"You've had a face like a slapped arse all day," Andy corrected me.

"Didn't you hear me?" Chris said. "I can get four tickets."

It turns out, according to Chris, a family in his street had tickets but the dad had broken his leg in a work accident and was still in the hospital.

"They have coach seats booked too," he declared. "So everything is sorted."

Now he had our attention.

It was Andy who asked the question we were all thinking. "Have you actually seen the tickets? Are they real?"

Chris gasped at our distrust.

"I can go get the tickets right now," Chris insisted.

I said, "I'm not that bothered, I've seen us lose up there enough times over the years."

"So what?" they all said.

"If we didn't go to games because we might lose, we wouldn't go anywhere!" Andy told me.

"Anyway," Bal said, "I think we'll win, and I don't want to miss it."

"You think we will win away to Man United in the Cup?" I asked.

I was mopping up the remnants of the egg and beans with my fried bread and paying more attention to that than the insane wonderings of my good friend.

"Yes," Bal said, "I do. I've got a good feeling about it. And we're due a good Cup run."

I wanted to say that no team is 'due' a good Cup-run. It's not like the FA Cup has a duty to share its glory among all of its participants.

But Bal had planted the seed of doubt in my head and already it had taken root - What if we won, and I missed it? It would be a historic day, a reward for all the defeats that fans endure.

Games like those lived in the memory long after the losses have faded.

That 1976/77 season that I first saw us play Millwall in the Cup ended with a Tuesday night home game against Bristol City. Jimmy Hill, managing director at the club, intentionally arranged for the match to kick-off fifteen minutes late, and with fifteen minutes of the game to go, put on the scoreboard that Sunderland had lost. Both teams would stay up if the score stayed the same. We cheered every pass from both teams as neither side made too much effort to go past their halfway line and at the whistle, both teams celebrated survival together.

By 1978, I was going to games with Chris, Andy and Bal. We beat the European Champions, Liverpool, one-nil with Mick Ferguson, the bearded beast, lobbing a perfect volley over Ray Clemence in front of the West End. The Match of the Day cameras were there, no doubt hoping to see a hatful of Liverpool goals, but instead they were treated to a brilliant penalty save from Jim Blyth, keeping out the 'Penalty King' Phil Neal. The unique camera-angle that preserved that brilliant penalty save came from a crane that had been raised high above the kop. Part of me idolised the likes of Kenny Dalglish, Graeme Souness, Emlyn Hughes and Ray Kennedy, but that day they were the vanquished opposition and we let them know it.

The same season we all went to two games in two days, losing away to Villa on Boxing Day and then a five-four victory at home to Norwich the very next day. To date, that is my only nine-goal thriller.

Two years later Liverpool were back and we sent them packing again by the same scoreline, this time defender Paul Dyson heading in the decisive goal.

In 1980, I learned a harsh lesson about following a team on a Cup run.

After smashing Watford 5-0 in a League Cup quarter-final replay, we were drawn against West Ham in a two legged semi-final. As the game approached, I started hearing the phrase 'all-ticket match', and up until that time, I had never bought a ticket for a game at Highfield Road. For any game all I had to do was turn up and paid my 50p at the turnstile. Now apparently, the first-leg was 'all-ticket', and it was 'sold-out'. By the time I realised, it was too late, and I missed it.

I had to settle for mum letting me stay up late on a school-night and watching the game on SportsNight without knowing the score. We started off disastrously and we were two-nil down in no time, including a calamitous own goal by my new hero Gary Thompson. After the build-up in the papers and on

TV and everyone in Coventry talking about the match, it was all over before half-time.

"I bet you're glad you didn't go now," mum said.

Close to tears, all I could hiss was, "Shut up, mum!"

Here was Lesson One for all Coventry fans: The waiting is the best part.

And then came Lesson Two: When there's absolutely no hope, sometimes Coventry City surprise you and come good.

In the second half, the game became a resurrection of biblical proportions and a miracle occurred. We scored three goals, including two from Thommo, and we won the game. It was a magical turn of events and from the depths of despair, the fans truly believed we could actually get to a Wembley final.

Before the second leg at Upton Park, which I again watched on SportsNight, our manager Gordon Milne said that from the kick-off time was running out for West Ham, who had to score to go through. But score they did through Paul Goddard after an hour and then, the knife in the heart, an eighty-ninth-minute winner by Jimmy Neighbour.

And that cruelly ended our dreams of a Wembley Final, albeit with the FA Cups little brother, the League Cup.

In 1983, we beat the European Champions (again) Liverpool four-nil and they were lucky to get nil. And in 1985, to stay in the First Division, we had to win our last three games and hope other results went our way. We won the first two and needed to beat the best team in England,and already-crowned Champions, Everton, at home. We destroyed them four-one, although to be fair they were severely hung-over from their celebrations, but all the same, we stayed up.

And for all of those games that I witnessed, I really expected us to win. At best, we were hopeful, but, to protect our sanity, realistic.

Which is why I had to go to Manchester United, just in case it turned out to be a rare good day.

"Alright, count me in," I said.

I was going to Man U away.

"Meet at the coach park at 9am."

I was actually glad I had something to take my mind off my other preoccupation.

I would like to say that later that day Coventry City buoyed my spirits by crushing West Ham at Highfield Road, but they didn't. We lost three-one and Tony Cottee scored a hat-trick.

Of course he did. He always did.

CHAPTER FIVE

Saturday 31st January 1987

I did love going to Old Trafford.

I loved huge stadiums and being part of a massive crowd.

Coventry City were a small tribe. Lads knew each other, if not by name or reputation, we just recognised each other. We'd see people on the West End or the Kop or Tomangos or The Three Tuns or Fishy Moore's or school. We didn't necessarily speak to each other, but we didn't have to. New people stood out, their credentials easily checked, not that we were being infiltrated by the CIA exactly, but we would spot outsiders before they could say 'You make me happy, when skies are grey'.

But Manchester United lads didn't have that advantage. The crowds at Old Trafford were so huge and their fan-base was country-wide, so local Man Utd lads couldn't spot away fans so easily. And we didn't want to be spotted.

Another reason I didn't mind Man United was that they were shit and they'd been shit for a long time. Despite their money and massive crowds, they hadn't won the League in my lifetime, done nothing in Europe and were relegated in the seventies (which we weren't). They won the FA Cup occasionally and sacked their manager every three years. Alex Ferguson who was finding that winning the Scottish First Division with Aberdeen was not the same as winning the English First Division. His solitary management skill seemed to be finding new excuses week-after-week and blaming anyone except himself. I'd bet any amount of money that he'd be sacked by the end of the season, and most Man United fans I knew hoped he would be too.

However, the reason I loved going to Old Trafford most was the market stalls that were set up outside the ground. They sold a massive range of T-shirts, hats and scarves and every era and every player was available. George Best, Denis Law, Sir Matt, and the celebratory FA Cup wins of '83 and '85. There was also plenty of uncensored terrace humour. But if you were lucky, some stallholders would drop the hinged-backboard of the stall and briefly reveal plenty of darker bad-taste stuff involving Leeds, Liverpool and Man City. There was also some non-football related stuff such as Chernobyl, Space Shuttle Challenger, Beirut, Hungerford, you name it. What they achieved in innovation was more than matched by their sick taste.

Busier than any market in the country, we could mix with the crowds and soak it up before making our way to the other end of the ground.

The pitch was half green and half white. Apparently, the Man United undersoil-heating, like ours, had broken down. The half of the pitch in the shadow of the stand was frozen solid, the other half had thawed.

From the start of the match, the mood in the Cov end was one of defiant resolve. We were going to enjoy our day out but expectations were low, a draw and a replay was our best possible outcome, even though we were above them in the league and our form at least as good as there's, if not better.

But we knew better than to set our hopes too high. We would always find a way to snatch defeat from the jaws of victory and, for our own sanity, it was best to protect ourselves with a healthy outlook of doom and gloom. For me, the news that

Dave Bennett was injured was catastrophic and meant that we'd be handed an even bigger hammering than I first feared.

However, as things turned out, I was wrong.

After 27 minutes, Keith Houchen managed to push the ball into the net with his nose after the longest goalmouth scramble ever. We went mental, me and Chris grabbing each other and surging down the terrace, fists punching the Manchester air, thrilled that we had scored.

Once we'd settled down, the bloke behind me summed up what supporting Cov was all about, "Typical!" he said, "We've scored too early. Now we'll get really hammered."

< < < <   > > > >

But we won. One-nil, thanks to that Keith Houchen goal. The striker had now gone from injury-prone liability to an actual living-legend in just one day.

I wanted to stay in the ground for as long as possible and soak up the atmosphere. The United fans were quick to leave, which meant I could look up on both sides of the stadium at tens of thousands of empty red seats. At the far end, almost empty but for a few stragglers, was the Stretford End. And we had silenced the forty-five thousand United fans and emptied this famous stadium.

I breathed in the air and savoured the silence, then made a dash for the coach.

Spirits were high on the way home. It was as if we'd beaten Liverpool or Barcelona away, not Manchester United, but it was good to go to Old Trafford and win for once.

We all sang about how Greg Downs had no hair and we didn't care, how there was only one Brian Burrows and that Brian Kilcline was six-foot-two, had eyes of blue and that he's after you. And we bounced along to 'George and John's Sky Blue army', belting it out for twenty minutes.

Once the sore throats and eardrums demanded a break, we settled down to discuss the match. The feeling amongst us was that we weren't a bad team this season and we were now into the last sixteen of the FA Cup. We'd all be glued to Radio Two on Monday to hear the draw for the fifth-round, and we fancied anyone at home. Arsenal, Tottenham and Everton were all in the hat with us and I personally wanted to avoid those three, but anyone else, home or away, would be fine.

< < < < > > > >

"I told you we'd win," Bal beamed, grabbing my arm and ruffling my hair.

"You did," I said, swatting his hand away. I had to hand it to him, he was right.

Bal's smile stretched ear-to-ear, "Who knows now-"

"Don't say it!" I warned him. "Don't even think it!"

"Yeah but-"

"No!" I snapped. "You'll jinx it."

Bal sealed his lips and his smile deflated.

We both knew, whatever we thought or hoped for, we couldn't say it.

Bal dropped into the seat, simmering with frustration.

He had my sympathy, but rules are rules.

I nudged his ribs and said, "I wonder who we'll get in the draw."

"We're in the fifth-round of the Cup," he gasped. "Can you believe it?"

I snuggled back into my seat, reliving Keith Houchen's goal and each time I relived it the ball took longer and longer for him to finally push it into the net. It was like the ball was a balloon rotating and floating in the air, just out of his reach.

The noise was ratcheting up. Everyone was talking, shouting, and songs were breaking out again, left, right and centre.

"Steve," Bal said.

"Yeah," I said.

He was sitting arms folded, eyes closed, and his enormous grin was back.

"Sometimes you have to let yourself dream."

As we passed Fort Dunlop, after booing at Villa Park, I settled into my seat, pulled my hat down over my eyes and took a moment to myself.

I'd been close to missing the game, certain that we'd lose, but, luckily for me, the lads had changed my mind. And as I replayed the highlights of the day, there was one thing that kept coming back to me. It wasn't Houchen's goal, although it had been brilliant, and it wasn't the final whistle that confirmed that we had won. It was what Bal had said.

"Sometimes you've got to let yourself dream."

Maybe he was right.

I talked a good game, but I never really dreamed big when it mattered. For some reason, I always held something back.

I felt in my pocket for some change and found at least five ten-pence pieces amongst a fist full of shrapnel.

Now, I thought, it's time to ask Question Five.

< < < <   > > > >

The coach slipped off the M6 at junction three and made its way into town. Eventually, we came to a halt in the coach park at Pool Meadow and I dashed through the underpass to the phoneboxes on the bus station side.

I dived into the first one in the row, stacked my five ten-pence-pieces on top of the grey box and dialled my mum's number and prayed that she hadn't yet gone out.

'What time was it?' I wondered. I had no idea.

The handset had buzzed three times, unanswered.

Sometimes dreams come true, I kept telling myself, sometimes.

But what about this one?

I only wanted one dream to come true, just one!

My mum answered the phone after five rings.

"Hello?"

"Mum, it's me," I said, "I need a favour."

"Steve, we're just going out," she sighed. "Can it wait?"

"No mum," I was trying not to shout, but I needed to stress how important this was. "Please, just do this thing for me. It will take two minutes."

"Steee-eve," she whined. I could imagine Derek standing there, looking at his watch and tapping his foot.

"Mum, I'm begging you," I said, "please."

"It'll have to wait," she told me, "we're already late."

"It's for a girl," I said as calmly as I could, "She's really nice mum, I think you'll like her as much as I do. She's going to turn me into a fully grown-up responsible adult, but only if I get to speak to her tonight."

"Well, why didn't you say so," she said. "How can I help?"

"Thanks mum," I said. "Open the phone book and look up the surname Morales."

The line was quiet for a few seconds and then I heard the pages of the telephone directory being flipped aside impatiently.

"How do you spell it?" Mum snapped.

"M.O.R.A.L.E.S"

Mum read out the names aloud as she, no doubt, ran her finger down the list, "Moragh, Moraida, Moraites, Moraitis-Jones, Moraity, Morales."

Result! "OK," I shouted, "Now can you look for Riverdale Close?"

"River what?" she said.

"Riverdale Close."

I silently prayed and waited.

I heard Derek say something and mum shushed him.

Two seconds passed. I could hear my mum breathing into the mouthpiece on the other end of the line. Then she drew a quick breath and said, "No, sorry, there's no Riverdale Close. Oh, wait a minute."

"Mum, is it there?"

"Yes, I nearly missed it," she laughed, "It was the very last one!"

"Thank you mum, you're a lifesaver. Can you read it out?"

I picked out the best empty cigarette box from the floor and retrieved a match from the ashtray. As mum read out the number, I scratched them into the inside of the fag packet with the ash of the match.

Then I asked mum read them again so I could double-checked.

"Thanks, mum," I said, admiring my prize beneath the phone box light.

"They won, didn't they?" mum asked.

"Who?" I said.

"Who do you think? Coventry beat Manchester United. Did you go to the game or not?"

"Oh yeah, yeah, of course, yes, we won. It was pretty bloody brilliant, actually."

It wasn't like mum to pay much interest in the City, but it was a big result so I shouldn't have been that surprised.

"Well, you know Zoe's getting married?"

I was aware of this. Zoe was Derek's daughter, mid-twenties, a nice enough girl, but there had always been a divide between us.

"And you're going, aren't you, to the wedding?"

"Yes mum," I said. My plan was to put in an appearance, make the effort, nothing more.

"It's the sixteenth of May," she told me.

"OK," I said. I was going to add that she'd have to remind me nearer to the time, but now I had what I wanted, I didn't want to prolong the conversation any longer than necessary.

"Good," she said. "I'm glad you said that you're going because you being there means the world to me."

"I know mum," I said.

Then she said, "Especially as it's Cup Final day."

"What!"

< < < <   > > > >

I dialed the number with great care.

After each number, the round dial turned back at a terminal crawl.

It took all of my concentration to remember the next number in the sequence.

After the last number, there were two rings and then the click of the receiver being lifted. I said a quick prayer and pushed one of the ten pence pieces into the slot.

"Hel-low," Sarah pronounced the word as two separate syllables.

My heart was leaping around in my chest like it had seen a last-minute winner, bouncing around my ribs. I couldn't believe she had answered. I was expecting to have a negotiation with her dad.

"Hi," I said. "It's me. Steve. The Movies To You guy."

"Oh hi," she said.

"Hi, how are you?"

"I'm good," she said.

"I'm sorry to bother you, but I have one more question."

"Ask away," she said.

"And just so you know, it's the most important question I have asked anyone in my whole life. So you may wanna sit down and take a moment to consider your answer."

"OK," she said, "I'm ready."

"So, the question is - Will you go out with me?" then I added, "Please?"

She didn't answer for a second, and I held my breath.

Then she said, "How do you know I don't have a boyfriend?"

"I'm sure you do, but it's best if it's just you. Might be awkward if there's three of us."

She laughed, "Well yes, but things aren't that simple, are they?"

It wasn't in a 'No' kind of way, more of an 'if only' sort of way.

"I know, it's complicated, but I reckon we can work it out," I said. "Somehow."

"I would but I can't-"

"Did I mention you'll have a great time?"

"I can't-"

"Yeah you can," I soothed, "it'll be fun!"

"OK, listen," she said. "I have a better idea. What are you doing on Wednesday night?"

CHAPTER SIX

Wednesday 4th February 1987

On Wednesday night I was back at Sarah's, by her request, but as she made clear, not on a date.

On the phone she'd asked me 'Do you have a business plan?' to which I obviously replied, 'Yes'.

'Bring it,' she'd said.

I assumed this was some kind of American rah-rah-cheer-leader type of encouragement, but she actually meant an actual plan put down on paper.

I parked the van on the road, not wanting to take up a spot on the gravel next to the Beamer or the Golf GTi, in case the missing Toyota returned home Goldilocks-style.

We were in the kitchen again, only this time Sarah sat beside me. I felt like I was at the Oscars.

She was wearing a white sweatshirt with UCLA on the front, cut short, just above her belly button. Her jeans were quite baggy and had elastic seems at the heels. Both fashion items were new to me. A big plastic clip held her hair back in a thick unruly bunch. As we spoke, she would release the clip, gather her hair and re-apply it, which reminded me a lot of my mother and her ponytail.

We had a pad of A3 paper in front of us and Sarah held a pen poised to start.

"OK," she said, "bear with me here, but as I'm studying to be a business-adviser, I thought we'd make a good team for taking your 'Movies To You' venture forward. If you let me look at your business, I can try to help you. We both come out winners."

I agreed wholeheartedly.

"The thing is, I can see that your business model targets a specific market," she said, "but to diversify your clientele the model will need to be adjusted to suit."

"Diversify?"

"More affluent areas."

"Posh people?" I asked.

"Yes."

I lent closer and whispered, "People round here?"

She nodded and smiled.

This was fun.

"Now," she said, "when approaching the 'new clientele'," swivelling her head in a circle and lip-syncing 'posh people', "we need to maintain the core USP, but adjust the marketing strategy to suit. Let's label them 'More Affluent'."

"What's a USP?" I asked.

"Unique Selling Point," she said, "and ours is-?" She gestured for me to fill in the blanks.

"Videos?" I said.

"Yes, but what's unique about 'Movies To You'?"

"We deliver movies to your house?"

"No," she said, "what's unique about it. That's why you are so smart. You provide a unique service."

My ego appreciated that little massage.

"And what's the current marketing strategy?"

I was determined to do better, but she was so gorgeous I couldn't concentrate. I tried to focus on the blank A3 paper pad and remember the book I had once read on marketing.

"OK, marketing, attracting customers, OK," I said. "Well, we park the van in a road somewhere, play loud music and knock doors and ask people if they want a video."

"Excellent answer," she said and started writing a summary of my answers on the left-hand side of the pad.

Marketing Strategy Current

Park van

Play loud music

Knock on doors

She wrote fast and her handwriting was extremely tidy.

"So," she said as she wrote 'Marketing Strategy Two' on the right-hand side of the page. My side. "Do you think that strategy will work with the 'More Affluent' clientele?"

"It worked with you," I said, and gave a grin.

"Well," she blushed, "You got lucky."

"I did, didn't I? Very lucky."

She blushed but ignored what I had said.

"So let's assume that the majority of the customers in the More Affluent market are not unlikely to fall for your boy-ish charms. Do you think honking your horn is the optimum strategy?"

"Probably not honking, no."

"OK, good."

"Loud music?"

"No."

"And knocking doors?"

"No."

"Right, so, we need another approach, but we keep the same USP-"

"Unique Selling Point," I chipped in.

"You got it," she said. I looked to her for approval and her eyelashes fluttered twice.

Oh my God, I thought, how does she do this?

"So we need to be unobtrusive when we make our initial approach. In fact, in all areas of the business, we need to minimise face-to-face interactions. We need to distribute written material, introductory fliers, catalogue lists, an explanation of our business process, everything."

I agreed.

"And our pick-ups and drop-offs need to be discrete. And we need to set up accounts, provide credit and arrange payments at regular but infrequent times."

As she spoke, she wrote on the right side of the page, which was my side. Her perfume drifted over me. I wondered if she wore it knowing that I was coming. And I wondered if she could smell my Blue Stratus.

To my joy, we had two more 'business strategy meetings' and by then we put our plan into action. We had estimated that there were two hundred houses within our target market, so we were going to print out three hundred fliers and labelled each one with a "call-time". This was the crucial factor of the strategy, Sarah explained. Customers would know exactly when they were to arrive with their mobile delivery service.

"More or less," I added.

"No, not more or less," she said. "Down to the minute."

"We never know how long each customer is going to take to choose a movie," I explained.

"Unless they've already made their choice."

"And how-"

"They choose from a list on the back of the flier."

"And what if they all choose the same film?"

"They won't," she said, "We'll have different lists with different movies."

I had to hand it to her. It just might work.

We had agreed on the three separate movie lists and the design and wording of the fliers. Each movie on the list had a tick-box next to it. The customer would tick the box, or boxes, of the films they wanted and the more they requested, the cheaper the price per item. She got a box of them printed up at Uni. We physically added the addresses to two hundred of them, all according to Sarah's 'locality strategy', which she colour-coded on a map.

My job was to amass the video cassettes themselves. So at some expense, I printed a number of professional looking labels and spent a week pirating multiple copies of the original movies.

The following Wednesday evening we delivered our fliers. If customers wanted a movie, they were to tick the box and place the flier in the outside of their letter box. We would then be able to visibly check each house and post the films through the letterbox with the payment details.

"We'll keep your trust system," Sarah has said. "That was what impressed me the most as a customer."

By the following Wednesday, we were ready to go. It had only taken three weeks from start to finish.

"I have one more stipulation," I said.

"What's that?"

"You estimated that from two hundred houses we could expect a response rate of ten percent for our first week, with an average spend of £1.42," I said.

"That is correct."

"So the target takings for week one is £28.40?"

"Yes."

"So my only stipulation is that if we make £30, we go out on a date."

She stared at me blank.

"Because I think you're pretty damn incredible to be with," I said.

Her expression didn't change.

I was getting worried.

"Deal?" I asked.

"Deal," she said.

And she smiled.

On the Thursday night, me and Sarah had retraced the steps we had taken to post our video-fliers looking for takers. We parked the van and covered a few streets on foot. There were some takers, but less than the ten percent I needed for my date to come into effect. Three of the takers requested four films though and one ordered five, so towards the end of the trail we were totalling over twenty pounds. We were going to be short of the required thirty pounds, but then something strange happened; we were accosted in the street.

Two middle-aged ladies approached us with fliers in their hands.

"Are you the mobile video people?"

I guess the graffitied logo on the van was the give-away.

"We were afraid we'd missed you," they said.

They both took two movies each.

"I know we said we wouldn't," Sarah said, "But maybe we should drive round and park up in each street for a few minutes? Adjust the plan?"

"Yeah, maybe we should."

And we did. And more people came out and said they thought they'd missed us.

Back in Sarah's kitchen, we totted up the orders, which came to £42.83.

We were both all smiles.

"So," I'd said, "I'm thinking Saturday night?"

She nodded.

"It's a date," I'd said.

CHAPTER SEVEN

Saturday 21st February 1987

It was six o'clock on Saturday. I was picking Sarah up at eight. Me, Bal, Andy and Chris were safely back in the car somewhere in Stoke, but when Bal turned the ignition key, the engine responded with a dull whine.

"Uh-oh," Bal sighed.

I was in the back with Andy.

"Don't do this to me, Bal mate."

"It was you who said you didn't want to go on the coach," Bal said back.

I'd told them about my big night, although not the stipulation that had brought it about, and that taking the coach would take too long. After a lot of moaning and complaining, Bal had offered to drive, and I offered to pay for the petrol.

Bal had a Mk3 Ford Escort, a marvellous piece of machinery, but had turned up in his brother's Vauxhall Viva Estate, which was a complete rot-box of a car.

"They'll know from the number plate that the Escorts from Coventry and they'll trash it, but no one's gonna key this. It's already wrecked."

He wasn't wrong.

The foot-wells on the passenger side were riddled with rusted holes, if you lifted the floor mats, you could see the road. The tyres were bold, one worn down to the canvas, and the brakes were down to the metal. The dash lights didn't work, but, as Bal pointed out, that didn't matter too much as the speedo didn't work either.

"It's got the same mileage as when he bought it," Bal laughed. "It's only got two months MoT left and it doesn't go over forty miles per hour, but Stoke's not far so it won't be a problem."

Or so he had said, but now it seemed there was indeed a problem.

After wiggling the gear stick for some reason, Bal tried to the ignition again, but again the car whined with decreasing enthusiasm.

"We'll have to bump start it," he told us.

"Great!" Chris sighed.

"Remind me why we didn't go on the coach," Andy said to me. "I hope she's worth it."

"And, Steve, it looks like you're gonna be late for your date after all," Chris said.

Chris was right. I was going to be late for my first proper date with Sarah. If we could get the thing started at all.

The lads could take the piss all they wanted, but it wouldn't make me feel any worse.

Me, Chris and Andy gathered at the back of the car and picked a spot of the fragile bodywork with which to get the thing moving.

The three of us got the giggles at our predicament and the fine balance of fate we found ourselves in.

I looked at the incline that sloped away in front of us and hoped that it would give us enough momentum to get up to a decent speed.

"Ready?" Bal shouted from the driver's seat.

"Ready," I confirmed.

"After three," Andy said.

"Need a hand, lads?"

We glanced across to see Six Stoke fans walking past. None of them looked happy or particularly keen to help.

"We're OK," I said and then added, "Three!"

We pushed.

The car crept forward.

We were getting up to a walking pace when I heard the Stoke fan say, "Good luck getting that going."

"Thanks," Chris replied, "And good luck next season."

"Chris! For fuck's sake!" Andy said as we got up to a bit of jog and the car picked up speed.

"Where you goo-in, lads?" the Stoke fan asked.

"We're goo-in to 'anley, duck, 'ow 'bout you?" Chris shouted.

"Cheeky bastards!" one of them yelled and without looking back I guessed they were now in pursuit.

"Pop the clutch!" I told Bal.

"Not yet," Bal called, "C'mon! A bit faster! Faster!"

"No! Now!"

As the car picked up pace running down the slope, we felt it moving away from our hands and I took a glance behind us.

Chris was now sprinting past me, and the six Stokies were about twenty yards behind him.

"Coventry bastards," one was screaming and threw something at us, but his aim was woefully astray.

I didn't have time for this!

I ran toward the car and could only watch and pray as Bal pops the clutch. The back of the car lurched up, like it had been shot in the hind legs, but then the back dropped down and plumes of smoke exploded from the exhaust as the engine sputtered into life.

We piled into the car and Bal floored the accelerator as we slowly made our getaway.

If there had been any trouble, it would have been down to him not being able to keep his mouth shut, but it wasn't my place to say anything. What's done is done. And all that matters is that we stuck together. None of us went to football to fight, but just by going we were taking the risk that of being involved in some kind of violence, some of it serious.

Once we'd safely navigated the streets of Stoke and were back on the Southbound M6 at Junction 15. It was six-fifteen. I managed to relax a little.

I estimated at least an hour to get back to Coventry with a top speed of forty, which was just enough time.

The game had been superb even though we had played terrible. In a cup-tie all that matters is the result, and although we didn't deserve it, we got the result we wanted. The only chance I could remember us creating was our goal. Even then, when Houchen's cross and landed at the feet of Dave Phillips, he miss-controlled it and had no choice but to side foot it to Mickey Gynn.

When Gynny slammed the ball into the bottom corner, the seven thousand City fans went berserk.

< < < <   > > > >

We had twenty minutes of hanging-on to endure and I was certain that we'd concede. We'd held out against Man United, but lightning didn't strike twice in the same spot, so we weren't going to do it again. We were missing both Lloyd McGrath and Dean Emerson in midfield, both suspended, and it showed. The longer the game went on, the more certain I became an equaliser was inevitable.

Stoke had a good penalty shout, not given, and one chance at the death; their striker went through and got a shot past Oggy at the other end of the ground. In that nanosecond that the ball flew goal-ward, I was assessing our chance in the replay, but the ball went wide of the net and we survived.

"Yes!"

Not long after that, the referee blew for full-time.

We all heaved a sigh of relief and a nervous laugh.

Andy smiled and said to me, "When your name's on the Cup, those things go your way."

I laughed.

That was the first time I actually allowed myself to consider that we would be in the quarter-finals, two games away from the final.

One more win and we'd be in the semi's.

And then, who knows?

Anything is possible.

I still couldn't allow myself to think of us having a day in the sun, Wembley in May, Abide With Me, rewriting the history books, dreams becoming reality. But that happened to other teams, it didn't happen to us.

You'd think I'd learn, I told myself.

After the game, they kept us in the ground for twenty minutes or more until the police decided it was safe for us to leave.

Crowded underneath the terrace. Most of us were restlessly cheerful, keen to get home and start the celebrations. At the start there were plenty of moos and bahs, but after ten minutes, even the farm animals got impatient.

Didn't the police chief know I had a hot date? Was he a bitter Stoke fan or a pathetic jobs-worth? I was ready to run with the bulls if need be. I just wanted to get out!

The gates eventually slid open and we spilled onto the empty streets. The four of us kept our heads down and headed for the car that wouldn't start and our minor run-in with the locals.

< < < <   > > > >

From what we could hear of Radio Two in the car, the last eight was us, Arsenal, Wimbledon, Leeds, Wigan and Tottenham. Walsall, Watford, West Ham and Sheffield Wednesday had all drew.

Ironically, we passed the turnoff for West Brom, the place where I had last seen Cov in a quarter-final in 1982.

I was about fourteen and had spent the entire week throwing at a picture of their striker, Cyril Regis (Yes, he of current god-like status at Highfield Road, but back then he was the Baggies centre-forward). I told myself if I could cut the picture in half by darts alone, fate would reward my persistence with a City win. After giving it a good try, by the Friday it was proving impossible to hit the last remaining linkages of the perforated paper, so in a rage I attacked it with all three darts in hand, stabbing it over and over. When that proved too difficult, I just ripped it down and, obviously, having failed in my task to steer fate, we lost two-nil. And Mr Regis scored an absolute screamer. The second goal, which I was perfectly in line to see, was the flukey deflection of Jim Hagen's chest that crawled over the line as Jim Blyth could only watch in horror. All my fault. We were never at the races, and it taught me another harsh lesson. Someone has to lose and when you want it most, it's usually you.

<< << >> >>

We turned off at Junction 3 at half-seven and as I gave a sigh of relief, the engine started sputtering.

Once again, Bal gave us an 'Uh-oh'.

The car ploughed on, much like a tractor, but not as fast.

We were on Foleshill Road with a line of cars convoyed behind us.

No one spoke so as not to jinx the bitch of a car that may have been terminally ill, but wasn't giving up without a fight.

<< << >> >>

I leaned forward and tapped Bal on the shoulder. "Any chance you could drop me off first in Cannon Park?"

Bal looked at me in disgust. "No chance! That's the other side of town."

"Cheeky bastard!" Andy said to himself. "First, he ditches us for a bird, now he wants us to go out of our way for him."

"Well, he needs to get laid," Chris said.

I sat back in the seat and muttered, "Wankers."

Chris and Andy chuckled away, enjoying my dilemma.

I could probably walk it in an hour. I estimated Bal's knackered Viva would get us there in twenty minutes, barring a breakdown.

With little choice, I sat back and watched the streets of Coventry slide by.

We got to Coundon and dropped Andy first.

"Cheers Bal, top man!" he shouted as he piled out of the car. "See you later guys, yeah. Enjoy. And Steve, don't do anything I wouldn't do!"

The car trundled on to Earlsdon to drop Chris off. He punched me on the arm and said, "Have fun, ya dirty bastard."

"See ya Chris."

I got out of the car and went to the boot and where I'd earlier stashed my sports bag.

"What you doing?" Bal said as I got into the back of the car.

"I'm getting changed. What does it look like?"

"I've seen it all now," he said and gently put the car in gear.

"No peaking!" I ordered, and unzipped my bag.

I had Bal drop me off at Sarah's house. I was bang on time. She was waiting at the door when I rang the bell. She was wearing all black; a rah-rah skirt, an oversized fluffy jumper and a baggy leather jacket. If she thought I smelled, she didn't mention it.

We caught a bus into town and Sarah talked non-stop the whole way there. She had a big project at Uni. Her older sister was pestering her about what was going on with me. Her dad was being as protective as ever and her mum had been ill again.

We got off the bus in Corporation Street. I asked her where she wanted to go.

"Can we just walk around for a while?"

"Sure," I said.

We did some window shopping and talked some more on the subjects of TV and music.

Most of the music she mentioned were American bands like the Bangles and Blondie, and some of the TV shows she liked I hadn't even heard of, but I nodded anyway, as she was in full flow.

Strangely, none of our selections seemed compatible. On the surface we had nothing much in common but as we dug deeper, we found we felt the same way about most things.

'We share the same core values', was how she put it.

"The movie I watch the most is probably 'Arthur'," I said. "It makes me laugh every time I watch it."

"It's OK," she said.

"I'll admit, it's not as funny as 'The Life Of Brian'."

"Isn't that like all stupid jokes," she said. "I don't get it."

"Seriously?"

"Yes, seriously."

"Sarah," I said, "I can't allow this."

We were standing outside Woolworth's by the market. She was looking at me with her doe-eyed expression and trying not to smile.

"But it's not too late," I went on. "You can still be educated. We can watch it together, and you'll see. It's the funniest film ever made, and ever will be made."

"I've seen it," she said, "I just didn't find it-"

"Don't say it! Please, do not say that The Life Of Brian is not funny."

She rolled her eyes in a huge weeping arc that felt to me like the sun's life-giving rays had shifted away from me, and then returned for me to bask in.

"The only time I laughed was when they said he was a very naughty boy."

"Oh my God!" I gasped, "Sarah, do you know what this means?"

"It means I didn't like the film that much."

"No," I said, and took both of her hands in mine. "No, no. This means…"

"What?"

"This means you might-" I looked away and shook my head. "I hope I'm wrong, I really hope I'm wrong."

"What?" she grinned. "I might be what?"

"I promise I'll still respect you, no matter what, but," I paused for effect, then said, "You might not have a sense of humour."

She laughed. "Well, how can that be true?" she said, "I'm going out with you, aren't I?"

Touche!

But at least, it seemed, we were going out.

We'd spent most of the evening sat on a bench in the Lower Precinct, talking. Neither of us wanted to go anywhere. Without saying it, we were happy just to talk.

For the rest of the night, we walked around some more, watched the escapades of the more dramatic relationships and going's on, and eventually headed back to Riverdale Close.

< < < < > > > >

It was gone midnight when we walked along Warwick Road from the train station to the War Memorial Park.

Sarah didn't seem cold.

If she had even mentioned being chilly, I would've slipped my arm around her, but she didn't. Much to my disappointment.

We walked slow, proper ambling at the slowest pace two people could walk. It felt to me like we were completely alone, that the buses and cars that passed us by didn't know that we were there and drove by oblivious. Even the people we passed, cosy couples and blokes with their hands in their pockets walking past, didn't seem to notice us.

I loved that I had the full attention of someone that I wanted to get to know. Every detail was critical, every slight nuance of her taste was fascinating. The movies, TV, food, music, holidays, everything she liked was completely compelling.

And Sarah seemed the same way about me. She wanted to know what I thought, what I wanted, what I missed. She wanted to know about me.

She'd enchanted me all night. Everything she did was both beautiful and different. In the chip shop when I asked her what she wanted, she said, 'I don't want anything, I'll just eat half of yours.'

So I bought a pickled egg, and she hated it, but she ate her half.

We'd been into town and had gone nowhere. I suggested we go for a curry at the Taj Mahal, but Sarah claimed she wasn't hungry. She also confessed that she had never had a curry.

"Not a real one," she qualified.

"You should try the Taj Mahal," I said. "That's about as real a curry as you can get."

"Will you take me sometime?"

I nodded, "Yeah, alright."

I didn't mention that I lived above the place. I thought it best to save that conversation for another time.

"How come you don't have an actual job?" she asked. "Or are you studying and working at the same time?"

I chuckled at that. "No, I'm not studying," I said, "I'm working for myself, building something from the ground up."

"I see," she said. "Interesting."

"Well, I've got my plan all worked out. I'm going to expand my video business, get more vans and hire people to do the rounds, do the whole of Coventry, then move onto the next thing."

"So what is the next thing?"

"It'll probably something to do with music," I said, "either management or production. I'm looking at computer games too. They're not my kind of thing really, but my mate's brother showed me this game he'd written and I can see it taking off in a big way. I've got a deal with this guy on Cov Market and he's looking at it. If he likes it, we'll be in business."

"Quite the entrepreneur, aren't you?" she smiled, seeming genuinely impressed.

"Well, you know," I said, "this ain't a rehearsal, is it? This is the real thing and I've got my plan to get where I'm going by the time I'm thirty-five."

"Why thirty-five?"

I shrugged, "Seems like enough time."

She laughed. "And what then? Retirement?"

"I'm not sure," I said. "I haven't thought about it."

"You want to reach your goals by thirty-five, but haven't thought about what you'll do after that?"

"I haven't got anything planned is what I mean."

I wasn't sure if the conversation had derailed or if I'd said the wrong thing, but when I glanced at her, she smiled naturally and I stopped worrying. We walked on for a while longer.

She'd semi-confessed that she'd gone to Blue Coats for Girls, an exclusive private school, and had stayed on for sixth form. Now she studying Commerce and Psychology at Lanchester Polytechnic, 'next to the cathedral', she explained, although I knew where 'the Lanch' was.

"Then what?" I asked.

"'Then what', what?"

"What are you going to do? After university."

"Well, my parents want me to go into beauty, hair design, or maybe retail."

"But you're doing Commerce and Psychology?" I said.

"I know, but they don't think I'm suited for business."

"I'm pleased for them," I said, "it's good they have a clear decisive plan, even if it's not for them."

She smiled and was quiet for a moment.

"I know what you're saying," she said, "but my parents are old-fashioned that way."

I wanted more than anything to reach out and hold her, but it wasn't time yet. I had no choice but to reach her with words. Or, at times like this, with no words.

"My dad's quite intimidating," she said. "He likes to help, but he ends up taking over. He's achieved so much in his life, he came from nothing. He was a boxer, the best in Guatemala. He fought in the Olympics and only lost four fights out of a hundred. During the revolution, he says a young man had to pick a side, and he chose the Revolutionary Party. They won the election in 1966, the year I was born. My dad had helped the American Government work with the Secret Army and a group called White Hand, Mano Blanco, to fight the Communists."

"Your dad worked for the Government?" I asked.

"He doesn't talk about it."

We walked a little longer, then she said, "When I was ten, there was an earthquake in Guatemala. Twenty thousand died, and the people blamed the government for not helping the survivors. I don't remember much about it but I remember the actual earthquake happening and the buildings where we lived were destroyed and people were living on the street."

"Oh my God."

"And then we moved to the US, first New York and then Denver."

"How long did you live there?"

"Eight years. I was fourteen when we came here."

"And now Coventry," I said. It seemed an incredible story. "Why here? Why not London or Australia?"

She shrugged. "My mum's from here. We used to come visit on holidays."

"You came to Coventry on holiday?" I laughed.

"We did."

She was silent for a while, then said, "My dad doesn't talk much about what he did, but we know he achieved a lot, first as a boxer, then in his work."

"It sounds like your dad is a tough act to follow."

She nodded. "I don't want to disappoint him, but-"

"You'd never do that," I told her. "He'll never be disappointed in you. If you decide to take a different direction in life than the one he had planned for you."

She stopped walking and stared at me. "Do you think so? Really?"

I thought I saw the start of a tear welling in her eye, but instead she blinked and it was gone, replaced by a strong will, self-control. But she was waiting for an answer.

"Yes, I think so," I said. "What matters is what you want. Good parents give their kids the strength to figure out what they want and go for it, even if the parents don't particularly like it."

"Do you think so?"

"Of course, and they'll be so proud of you when you show them you have what it takes to make your dreams come true."

"I hope so," she said.

The wind got stronger at the edge of the park. I looked up at the sky. It seemed impossibly dark. There were no stars or moon, the sky was a pure blackness that stretched out forever endlessly.

She looked at me and smiled. "This is like a stolen first date."

I had kind of thought that it was a first date but wasn't sure where the 'stolen' bit had come from, so I said, "It does."

"I've never had a stolen first date before."

"Me neither."

I had to consciously not stare at her the whole time, but I didn't want to miss a second of this. I wanted to feel every emotion, every expression, every second that we had together.

I was about to try a line like 'every stolen date should be sealed with a stolen kiss', but as I formed the sentence in my head, she grabbed my arm and I thought she was about to kiss me. My heart leapt up and blocked my throat, but then she lifted her leg and I realised she using me to keep her balance.

"Stone in my shoe," she said as she shook the offending article.

I could feel her grip on my arm, and the shifting weight of the body as put her shoe back on and let go of me. My heart was racing faster than it ever had before. It was racing so fast that I was worried that it would just stop.

I need to be careful, I told myself. If she can nearly give me a heart-attack by touching my arm, I could be in serious trouble here.

We walked again.

"We're breaking all the rules, aren't we?"

"Rules aren't for the likes of us," I said, "that's why it's so much fun when we break them."

"I like breaking rules with you."

"Me too."

"Are you okay?" she asked.

"Yeah, I'm fine."

"Good, because I need to know if ever you're not fine."

"OK."

"I'm serious. Will you promise me?" She looked at the pavement at our feet as she asked me this. Her hair had fallen like a veil to cover her face.

"I promise," I said.

"If anything happens that makes you not OK, or not fine, you promise to tell me?"

"Yes." I stepped toward her and she turned to face me, but kept her head low. I put my arms around her and guided her head to my shoulder, rested my cheek on the top of her head and breathed her in.

And I got it. We were stealing dates. She had to deal with how she felt and how she would deal with the consequences because I knew enough about her and her world by now to know that there would be consequences. And they would be designed specifically in such a way that she couldn't defend and would hurt her the most.

"I promise," I whispered and held her tight.

The moon was now vaguely visible through the clouds.

Sarah hugged me back and we didn't let go for a long time. I couldn't see her face, but I knew her well enough to conjure her expression in my imagination.

And I knew what she was thinking.

'Is this for real? Because I need to be rescued and I can't rescue myself'.

After a while, she let go and looked up at me. She looked so beautiful in the dim orange glow of the lights. She looked like an angel in that darkness.

I wanted to kiss her. More than anything I've ever wanted to put my lips to hers, but we had an understanding now.

I'd made a promise.

And that was more important.

CHAPTER EIGHT

Tuesday 24th February 1987

"My parents and my eldest sister," Sarah said, "well, mostly my eldest sister, want to know who you are."

"Who I am?" I said, "I hope you lied."

"I did," she nodded. "No way could I tell them the truth."

"That I'm a jobless chancer and border-line criminal who wants to steal you away to a life of poverty, misery and despair?"

"Yeah, you got it in one!"

We'd been seeing each other about twice a week and had kept things very low-key, if not out-and-out clandestine.

We were in the Green Man in Kenilworth, a low-key hide-out. Coventry pubs were out of bounds since we came close to literally bumping into two of Sarah's college friends the previous week. We walked into The Three Tuns and they were at the bar. Sarah did a fast U-turn, grabbed my arm and dragged me out of there.

I guessed she was still seeing her boyfriend, which we never talked about, and I didn't even know his name, but I wasn't too thrilled that I had to be hidden away. It hurt even more to know that when she wasn't with me, she was probably with him. That burned me real bad. We were too early in our relationship for me to force the issue and I hoped she would raise it when she was ready.

"So what did you tell your sister?" I asked her.

She sipped her wine and looked around the room. Most of the people in the lounge were couples, probably all from Coventry and cheating on someone.

She sat back and took a breath, then made her announcement, "We're friends."

I nodded.

"So you're slumming it?"

"Massively!" she said, "You're a bad-boy trying to make his way out of the ghetto by any means possible."

"By renting videos? Not drug dealing or stealing cars?" I said. "And they bought that?"

"I'm an excellent actress," she sneered at me, "and they're a bit naïve about ghetto-life."

"The first rule of the Con Man is to 'Know your audience'. They're called 'marks', by the way."

"I know what a 'mark' is."

We were sat at the bar, she had her thick padded Parker jacket on with the fluffy fur lining like a lion's mane.

"Tell me about your parents," she said.

"Well," I started, and had to think for a second about how I did this.

"Have you told them about me?" Sarah asked, no doubt sensing my apprehension.

"I told my mum," I said. "It was funny. I was at her house. We were in the kitchen, drinking coffee. And she just said, 'You look cheerful. When do I get to meet her?'"

"Your mum said that?"

"Yeah, that was the first thing she said, 'When do I get to meet her?'"

For some reason, Sarah loved that. Maybe it was a girl-thing.

"So when does she get to meet me?" she asked.

"I was thinking we could go for Sunday dinner," I said, "but be warned, you might've eaten in some fancy restaurants in your time, but even the best restaurants in the world are nothing compared to my mum's Sunday roast."

"Really?" she said, "So just how good is it?"

"It's life-changing," I said. "It takes everything you think you know about roast beef and expands it into a different universe. The only problem is that the ordinary world is never the same again. It's too normal, bland, dull, and it will be that way forever. Just one roast potato, just one, would bond with your taste buds do strongly that you would never forget that one potato."

"It sounds alright," Sarah said flatly. "Can you get me an invitation?"

"I'll see what I can do."

Sarah took a sip of her wine and carefully put the glass back on the table.

"Will your dad be there?" she said.

I knew it was coming. You get a sense for these things, and I had wanted to raise the subject myself, but I'd put it off and now it was here.

"My dad died when I was twelve," I said. "He had a heart-attack in his car. Unexpected."

"I'm so sorry," Sarah gasped, both of her hands went to cover her mouth. "I feel terrible for-"

"It's OK," I said, "I'm glad you asked me. I was going to tell, but-"

"You don't have to," she said, "if you don't want to."

"No it's fine," I said. "My dad was a bit of a character, by all accounts. He was a wheeler-dealer and supplied the market traders, so I'm always hearing tales about what he got up to."

Sarah nodded without speaking.

"He was a family-man too. Madly in love with my mum, and he was a great dad. He took me to the park, we went fishing, he took me to the football, we did everything together. He was great."

I ended it there. I had learnt to figuratively draw a line under the first conversation about this subject. It's a shock for people and it's best not to go on about it.

Sarah nodded, and we sat in comfortable silence for a minute or so.

"So does Coventry have a big game soon?" she said. "My brother said something about it."

"Yes," I said, "Sheffield Wednesday away, FA Cup Sixth Round."

Sarah nodded, then shrugged. "I didn't understand a word of that, except Sheffield, and it's on Wednesday."

"It's not on Wednesday," I laughed, not sure if she was winding me up. "They're called Sheffield Wednesday."

"Are you going?" she said.

"Yeah, of course," I said. "I'm not going to miss the biggest match we've had in years."

She did the nodding again, but said nothing. I recognised this as a signal that she was waiting to be offered something. I guess I was getting to know her.

"Do you wanna go?"

She faked thinking about it for a second, then said, "I'd love to! Thank you."

"It's on Saturday week," I said, "so you definitely want a ticket?"

"Can you get me one?"

"Sure I can."

She nodded. "Count me in."

"You going to the City game?" someone asked.

I turned around. The pub landlord was leaning on the bar and inserting himself into our conversation. He seemed a decent enough guy, but he wasn't backward in coming forward.

"Yes, we are," Sarah told him. "Steve can get tickets."

He shook his head, "Good luck with that, they're gonna be like gold dust."

"It's not gonna be a problem," I said.

"How are you getting there?" he asked.

"I don't know," I said, "on the coach, probably."

"Tell you what," said the landlord. "If you can get me three tickets, I'll give you a lift in the Wedding Car."

We both knew about the 'Wedding Car'. It was always parked in the pub garden, a gleaming white Jaguar XJ Sedan.

"That would be so cool!" Sarah grinned.

"Alright, so have we got a deal?"

Sarah looked at me, and I looked at the landlord. "Absolutely," I said. "Three tickets?"

"Three tickets," he said.

CHAPTER NINE

Saturday 24th March 1987

That Saturday was going to be a dream come true. I had tickets to an FA Cup Quarter-Final and a whole day with Sarah. We'd returned to The Green Man to finalise the Wedding Car deal and hand over the landlord's three tickets for the Leppings Lane terrace.

'I'll pick you up outside the Wyken Pippin at ten-thirty,' he had told us.

We smiled, and said, 'We'll be there!'

And we were.

But he wasn't.

"I never should've trusted him," I snarled.

We were outside The Pin. It was eleven o'clock.

"Maybe he's running late," Sarah said.

On a day of this magnitude thirty-minutes wasn't late. Thirty minutes late translated to 'not coming'.

"He stitched us up," I told her, "I never should've given him the tickets upfront."

"So how are we going to get there?"

I'd been trying to thumb a lift. Cars were streaming up Ansty Road with sky blue scarves hanging out of the windows. Every car looked full. Nobody was stopping.

I'd been to a phone-box and called Andy, Chris, Bal, and anyone I could remember the number of, but they'd all left.

"Maybe we could get the train," Sarah suggested.

"No chance," I told her, "all the trains are booked up, and we'd never get to the station in time, anyway."

"What about the video van?"

"Andy's got it," I said.

"So what are we going to do?"

"I don't know," I said, "I'm working on it."

I was out of ideas, apart from thumbing a ride, but the stream of cars was becoming a trickle.

I couldn't believe it. The biggest match in years, Sarah's first-ever game, and we were stranded in Coventry. I'd been to hundreds of games and never even missed a kick-off. It was a record I was proud of, and now this.

"I'm gonna kill him," I said. "I bet he planned to stitch us up all along."

"Maybe he had an accident or something," Sarah said.

I was furious, but even so, I didn't want to get into an argument.

Sarah sat on the wall and put her hands on her lap. "So what are we going to do?"

I wasn't ready to give up, but I had nothing else to offer.

A few minutes went by without us speaking and in that time I saw one car with City scarves flying from the back windows. I waved both arms to flag it down, but as it sailed past, I saw there were five people in the car. The guy in the passenger seat raised both hands in an apology and the driver tooted his horn.

That was our last chance, I thought to myself. I might as well throw my ticket down the drain.

But then, I heard another car horn blast, three proud and loud toots, that announced hope and rescue.

I traced the origin back to a minibus in The Pin car park. It drew me, trance-like, and I walked straight across the Ansty Road and nearly getting ran over in the process.

As Sarah arrived at my side, the driver of the van saw us, wound down the window and shouted the single most beautiful word I had ever heard in my life.

"Hillsborough?"

< < < < > > > >

"We're from The Pilot," the driver told us. "We've been round every pub in Coventry seeing if anyone needed a lift. The Pin was our last stop."

"Thank God we saw you," I said. "Our lift let us down."

"Unbelievable," said the lad in the opposite seat. "Who could do a thing like that?"

I shook my head in disgust, but I couldn't believe how lucky we'd got.

They had borrowed the bus from a local school, six twin-rows of seats. We had the two seats at the front, one older Irish gentleman making a show of donating his seat to "the young lassie" and reminding his friends to be on their best behaviour.

As Sarah had made her way to the vacated seat, he'd removed his hat and bowed with a flourish, like Walter Raleigh laying his cape down for the Queen. "Welcome aboard our merry vessel. It is my honour and privilege to be sharing your company on this most wondrous of voyages. I'm Gerry, these are my compatriots, and we are embarking on a most historic mission."

"Thank you so much." Sarah flushed red cheeks, not quite knowing what to make of the situation.

"The pleasure is all mine," Gerry assured her.

We took our seats and immediately Sarah wrapped her arm around my elbow and snuggled into me for comfort or protection.

As the van pulled out of the car park, someone tapped me on the shoulder and I turned round.

"I'm Dave," said the lad, "Beer?"

"Thanks," I said and took the can he was offering. "I owe you guys. I won't forget this. We'll have to meet in The Pilot for a-"

"Don't worry about it," said a lad at the back of the van. "We've got plenty." He nodded to a stack of Tennents Super.

"I think we've landed on our feet here," I said to Sarah.

She smiled but didn't speak. She looked nervous, not taking her eyes off the lads in the van, unsure how to act.

I offered her a swig of Tennents and she shook her head at first, but I insisted and she relented.

We hit the M69 just as the police spot-check was packing up. They were searching vans for beer, which, I imagine, they were confiscating.

"See that?" said Gerry. "That's the luck of the Irish, to be sure."

We raised our cans and the singing started.

< < < <   > > > >

For the next two hours we swapped stories of our City histories, key matches we'd been to, the good, the bad, and the bloody awful. I made sure Sarah wasn't excluded and the lads were all respectful and drew her out of her shell. Dave, the lad behind us who kept a steady stream of Tennents coming my way, chatted away with her about his marital issues for at least half an hour, the classic theme of which was 'she doesn't understand sometimes I want to be out with the lads'.

"Just tell her how you feel," Sarah advised, "but without getting too defensive, she'll understand."

"I'll try that," Dave said. "I must admit I get a bit shirty when she bangs-on about it."

Sarah nodded, a picture of sympathy.

The driver, Gary, shouted back to us, "We're about thirty minutes away. Gerry, give us a song."

"Yeah, come on Gerry," someone shouted.

"G'awn Gez," Dave added.

Gerry raised a hand in recognition and started searching his pockets for something. I thought he might be about to play a harmonica, but instead, he pulled out a hip flask and theatrically unscrewed the lid and took a swig.

"This is my magic singing juice," he told Sarah, slurring each word into the other. "One sip and I'm Daniel O'Donnell!" He offered the flask to Sarah, who laughed but declined.

"I'll try it!" Dave shouted, but Gerry batted away his outstretched hand with surprising dexterity and speed.

"Fagarf!" he snarled.

Gerry took another swig, then resealed the lid and slipped the flask back into a pocket. He took a deep breath and raised himself up, smiling at each of the attentive audience.

He cleared his throat with an 'Ah-hem!' and then he sang what sounded like an Irish sea-shanty.

"Oh, when I was a young lad, in the Emerald Isle,

I would dream of being a football star,

But not for Spurs or Ar-se-nal,

And all the pretty ladies,

would want to play with me,

Cos I was a football player for Coventry City."

We all cheered at the mention of the greatest team in the land.

Gerry went on.

"If I was a football player,

for Coventry City,

All the pretty ladies,

Would want to play with me,

And I would juggle my balls,

As they sit on my knee,

If I was a football player,

for Coventry City."

We were in hysterics, but he hadn't finished.

"If I was a football player,

for Coventry City,

All the pretty ladies,

would want to play with me,

I'd use my sliding tackle,

to make them so happy,

If I was a football player,

for Coventry City."

Gerry kept us entertained for the rest of the journey as we left the M1 and crossed the north of Sheffield. Before long, there were crowds on the streets making their way and police presence everywhere.

With the ground in sight, an officer stopped us and asked if we were Coventry as none of us had colours.

"We are," Gary said, and we were guided into a side road beside a railway embankment.

"Go down this road, all the way to the bottom, then turn round, head back, and park in this first spot you see. Do you understand?"

"Yes," Gary said.

"Right. Go!"

We did as we were told.

Once we parked and disembarked, Gary called everyone together except Gerry, who was telling Sarah a tale about his exploits of a night out in Buenos Aires when he was in the merchant navy.

"Listen," Gary said, "remember we promised Gerry's missus not to let him out of our sight. That means all day, during the game and after the game, until we bring him back here to the van. Understood?"

They all nodded.

Dave explained, "If we lose him, he'll go walkabout and won't be back for weeks. His missus will kill us, no joke."

"He'll be alright," Gary told me, "as long as we don't let him slip away."

"Hey, thanks again for picking us up," I said. "Without you, we'd still be in Cov."

"It's no problem," Gary said, "but listen, you need to get back here straight after the game, the cops will send us on our way and if you're not here, we'll have to go without you."

I nodded, "Understand. We'll be here."

"Alright, enjoy the game."

I turned to Sarah, who seemed fascinated, or petrified, by the sheer number of people making their way to the ground.

"Sarah," I said.

She turned to me, her eyes wide with excitement and expectation.

"We need to stick together, but just to be on the safe side, when we come out after the game, if we do get split up, make your way back here to the van, OK?"

She nodded. This was serious.

"It's not far to the ground from here, we stay on this main road, it's about ten minutes walk," I said. "On the way back, remember the railway bridge? That's your turn."

She was looking worried.

I counted the lamp posts between the van and the main road. "It'll be packed with people here when we come out, even more than there are now, so remember the van is parked by the fifth lamp-posts."

"Fifth lamp-post," she nodded.

"I promise I won't lose you," I said.

We started walking with the crowd, immediately dropping into that strong-paced pre-match marching beat.

"And," I said, "one last thing."

"What's that?"

I took her hand in mine and squeezed it.

"Don't let go."

She squeezed my hand back and momentarily swerved into me so our shoulders bumped together.

"I won't," she said.

< < < <   > > > >

The pavement to the ground was packed full of fans. Many spilled onto the road and more or less stopped the traffic, but the police didn't intervene. They just wanted us into the stadium as soon as possible. It was two-thirty, half an hour to kick-off. We were going to make it in plenty of time, but the terrace was going to be crowded, so we'd have to take the best spot we could.

Today was about being there.

Sarah clung to my hand and as we turned the corner Hillsborough Stadium came into sight.

"Is that it?" she said, marvelling at the stadium.

"That's it," I told her.

"I didn't think it would be so big," she said.

"It holds fifty thousand, one of the biggest in England."

"Will there be fifty thousand today?"

"Yep!" I said, "Full-house."

We took a left to get to the away end and it was all Cov. We could already hear the songs going up from the fans in the ground and the nerves were tingling up and down my back.

With all the drama of getting here, I hadn't thought about the actual game, but now it was almost upon us.

When we turned into Leppings Lane, I saw the turnstiles. It was a relief to see that the queues were only three or four deep. Within minutes we're through and into the area behind the stand and it was absolutely packed solid with fans. Nobody seemed to move, but everyone seemed to be heading toward a single tunnel about ten feet wide.

From the shouting voices, I knew it was going to be tight getting through and I didn't want to put Sarah through that ordeal. If you're not used to that kind of situation, it can cause serious panic and there's nowhere to go if that happens.

"This is crazy," I told her. "Let's hang back until the crowd goes down."

People were still pouring in through the turnstiles and pushing past us, eager not to miss the kick-off and soon the angry voices were drowning out the fans already in.

Although we tried to hang back, we were being pushed forward by the crowd and were moving toward the tunnel. Each time the crowd took a step forward we had to go with them.

"Keep moving at the front!" someone was shouting, "Keep moving! We can't move back here! Keep moving!"

Although we were trying to avoid the crush, we were getting dragged into it. I turned to look for the quickest way out, but behind us was as solid as it was in front. We couldn't go back now and the push from behind meant when you lifted your foot to take a step, it was difficult to find a spot to put it down.

I was constantly saying to Sarah, "You OK? You alright?" and she kept nodding, but she didn't speak. She looked petrified, and I didn't blame her. I tried not to let any panic show in my voice but in my mind, I was seeing all kinds of nightmare scenarios; one person losing their footing and falling, limbs breaking, bodies piling up by being forced off their feet from the pressure of the surge.

Maybe people on the other side of the tunnel were moving forward now because the crowd seemed to move through the tunnel faster, but that only made it feel more precarious.

Then, as the pressure eased, I saw someone moving across the crowd, shouting his 'excuse me's as he pushed through. At first, I thought he was eight feet tall, then I realised he was carrying his young son on his shoulders.

I used my arm to create a space for him and he gave me a look of eternal gratitude.

"This is madness," he shouted, barely audible above the screaming and shouting. He nodded in the direction he was heading as he drew level with me and stopped to say, "I'm sure there's a side entrance. I was here last season."

I nodded and made sure I had hold of Sarah as I prepared to follow him.

"Thank you," he shouted, and we fought our way across the crowd. People were happy to let us through so that they could step into the space we'd left. In what felt like only a few minutes we were out of the crowd and could push our way down the side of the brick wall at the back. As the crowd thinned out, we could breathe in deep lungfuls of fresh air. We turned a corner and unbelievably there was the Leppings Lane End Terrace laid out before us within easy reach of a few feet.

The guy with the lad on his shoulders let out an ear-piercing four-fingered whistle, and then as the heads of the crowd turn to us, he shouted "This way! This way! You can get through here."

I started shouting the same, waving people over and they hesitated at first, not believing that there was a clear entrance just a few yards away from a body-packed tunnel.

A stream of them followed us. I grabbed Sarah's hand again and we slipped through a few lines of standing fans to find a spot to watch the game.

"Is it always like this?" Sarah asked in all innocence.

I laughed, as much from relief as anything else. "Not always," I said, although I had never been so scared of the power of a mass of surging people.

"Are you OK?" I asked her.

She nodded, she seemed fine, her attention had turned to the sight and sounds around us, fifty-thousand people gathered into four sides of the stadium, all focused on the playing-field before them. The jam-packed spion-kop at Hillsborough was a sight to behold, a huge terrace matched only, dare I say it, by the vastness of Villa Park's Holt End. That stand alone held nineteen thousand, more than many grounds.

The North and South stands were also crammed and huge, not an empty seat in sight.

But it was the noise that was most impressive. Only when in huge crowds can the total noise drown the raised voices of those around you. The deafening hum of the thousands of voices was broken only when the team, in their changed yellow kit, emerged from the tunnel from the South Stand.

Every City fan immediately burst into cheers and raised hand-claps.

Sarah was taken by surprise and her eyes searched the scene for the cause of this reaction and when she saw the players approaching from the far end of the ground, she pointed and screamed with the rest of us.

Sarah turned to me, looking puzzled. "I thought they played in Sky Blue?"

"This is the away kit," I shouted, "because Sheffield Wednesday play in blue and white and that would be a colour clash."

I don't think she heard a word I said, but she nodded.

As the players kicked a ball around to warm-up, the crowd settled down into a group-hum of anticipation.

Sarah pointed to a few players saying, "Who's that?"

"Keith Houchen."

She pointed again.

"Greg Downs."

Then she shouted, "Dave Bennett, I know him."

I didn't know how the hell she knew who Benno was, in fact, I didn't want to know!

The anticipation boiled up into a roar as Killer dealt with handshakes and coin-toss and then the lads lined up to kick-off.

And we'd made it. We were here, the biggest game since that crushing disappointment of West Brom seven years before. My nerves were shaking throughout my body and not just because of the football.

I stood directly behind Sarah, slightly to her side so she could turn and talk to me, but also so I could put my arm around her waist. She leaned back against me and said, "Do you think we'll win?"

I laughed. She was so beautiful.

"I hope so," I grinned and she smiled in that perfect way.

Her brown eyes met mine, (like when you'd been looking for someone and then you see them and smile). I noticed how delicately her eye shadow and her shade of lipstick was so subtle it seemed invisible yet it enhanced her features beyond beautiful. When her lips parted by just the tiniest amount, I wanted to kiss her and I could see in her eyes that she wanted me to. I leant toward her. Then a shrieking blast from somewhere far away shattered the moment and she jumped and turned away.

The referee's whistle was met with the biggest roar of the day as the game kicked off and we, for better or worse, were in for the ride of our lives.

Sarah focused on the game for the first five minutes. She knew, like me, that I was about to kiss her and whatever she made of it, I did not know.

She hadn't slapped me, which was good, but she hadn't swooned with desire either.

My head was spinning from disaster to fantasy, but luckily for me, there was a football match going on in which I had a vested interest.

Naturally, I was immediately engrossed.

"C'mon City!"

I would repeat that little mantra every ten seconds.

I had to fend off the demons in my head telling me that Wednesday were about to score every time they crossed the halfway line. When they actually attacked the goal in front of us that threat was a very real and present danger. And if we did concede, the demons seemed to know, then the game was over as far as we were concerned. Our best outcome was a nil-nil draw and take our chances in a replay because we were Coventry City and as we all know, Lesson One: the waiting is the best bit. And the waiting was over.

We had a few moments to cheer though as we got into their box a few times, but at the far end of the ground, it was impossible to see if we created a chance or if Wednesday's defence had dealt with our threat comfortably.

Sarah threw me a glance and a smile about ten minutes in, but soon faced forward again. I leaned to her ear and said, "You OK?"

She nodded vigorously, but didn't turn round.

We'd definitely settled into the game and were giving them something to think about when we went forward, but our strength wasn't in dominating teams. We were better at soaking up attacks and hitting them on the break.

And so it was after seventeen minutes and a clearance was won bravely on the halfway line by Lloyd McGrath. He was absolutely clattered by a Wednesday player but got the ball to Big Cyril who laid it off to Benno and the break was on.

"Yes!" I snarled through gritted teeth as Cyril peeled away down the right channel and Benno skipped past his man.

I knew then that if Benno put Cyril through, then he would score. I literally knew it to be true. After all, I'd seen it before with my own eyes that day at The Hawthorns, when he did it against us for West Brom.

Of course, Benno delivered the perfect pass and Cyril was on to it.

Once he took his touch, I leapt into the air, fist punching the sky. "Yes! Cyril! Yesssss!"

One second later, fifteen thousand City fans joined me in the wildest celebration in our history.

It was mental, insane. All around us bodies surged toward the fence. I grabbed hold of Sarah as she turned to me and we hugged and jumped and screamed and I swear there was a tear in her eye when she looked at me and smiled and I knew the moment had arrived and we were suddenly frozen to the spot as my lips touched hers and hers parted slightly as she put her arms around my neck and I squeezed her gently close to me and we melted into our first kiss amid Sky Blue pandemonium. Her lips were so soft and her body was so warm, I felt like I could breathe her in and hold her there forever.

We got to half-time still in the lead and I spent most of the break staring into Sarah's eyes and stealing more kisses. Her voice was soothing, but my stomach was tying itself in knots. It didn't seem possible that these two things were happening at the same time. I reminded myself that neither one had actually happened yet, City were only halfway to the semi-finals and Sarah was still someone else's girlfriend.

It felt like too much to ask.

"Do you think we'll score again?" Sarah asked. She gave me a sly smile and a squeeze.

"I really, really hope we do!" I smiled and squeezed her back. "So are you a true Sky Blues fan now?"

She nodded. "I think I am," she said, "I could get used to this."

"I have to say, though, it's not always this good," I told her. I wanted to make a joke about how football is a cruel sport and we Cov fans had suffered more than our fair share, but things were so perfect I thought, for once, there's no room for pessimism, despite what my gut-feeling was telling me.

Twenty minutes into the second half and Cyril gets put clean-through one-on-one with the goalie, in other words, a certain goal, but the linesman flags and the referee gives offside (but never in a million years was he anywhere near offside). After fifty-seven minutes their keeper comes out forty yards to launch the free-kick into our box, which is fine because we've dealt with long balls all day long, right? But this time it bounces into the box and we don't deal with it and someone in a dark blue and white stripe shirt swings a leg and we see the net bulge and the kop erupts into a sea of arms. Gary Megson's ginger mullet is bouncing in front of them all and there's nothing we can do but stand there and take it.

I should've known. It dawned on me that this is the first goal we've conceded in the Cup. I start to think that if we'd lost at Stoke, Man Utd, or even at home to Bolton back in January, we'd have been over it by now.

Sarah looked genuinely saddened by this turn of events. I console her with a kiss on the forehead, but who's going to console me? Maybe I don't want to be, maybe I derive some masochistic pleasure out of building my hopes up for them to be destroyed.

But then the City fans start to rumble and the noise wakes me from my self-pity.

"C'mon City!" someone shouts from behind. Others repeat the cry. A roar emerges from fifteen-thousand voices that travels to the players as they line up to restart.

We trust in you! We know you can win this!

In the seventy-eighth minute, it became clear that the football gods were favouring us that day. If the phrase 'wicked deflection' didn't already exist, it would have been invented once Keith Houchen's took the ball into their box and tried his luck with a right-foot shot. He shot hard and low to the far corner. The keeper had it covered, but their defender took matters into his own hands. He stretched out his foot to block it. The ball, somehow, bounced up off the ground, flew over the keeper mid-dive and landed, very pleasingly, in the net. It was our turn to erupt again.

Whether we were emotionally exhausted or we all felt the same sense of fate (or confidence in the team), we all seemed to know at this point that we would win. All of my pessimism, doom, gloom and negativity disappeared and I was ready for the party to start.

Five minutes later, it did. Houchen was there again. He collected Dave Bennett's precision overhead forty-yard 'Hail Mary' pass from the back of Megson's mullet and stroked the ball firmly beneath the keeper and into the net.

Sheffield Wednesday 1 Coventry City 3.

The history-making result, made official when the referee blew the final whistle, was a mixture of mostly joy but also relief, not just the events of the last fifteen minutes, but all the years that Coventry fans had endured with no genuine success. It was so worth the wait.

We applauded the players as they celebrated in front of us again.

"We'd better get back to the van," I told Sarah. "We don't want to be stranded in Sheffield tonight."

She nodded and I grabbed her hand.

We'd shared an amazing experience, witnessed a miracle and there was now another date with destiny to look forward to.

As we hurried back to the van, clinging to each other as we were buffered along with the crowd, buzzing with excitement.

We were the first ones back. The others arrived in dribs and drabs and were greeted by hugs and cheers and tears. Grown-men or not, we had feelings too. We all had our tales to tell and highlights to share. We could now dream of Coventry City in an FA Cup semi-final.

Then someone said, "Guys! Where's Gerry?"

$$< < < < \quad > > > >$$

"I left him with you when I went for a piss!" Dave shouted.

"He said he was going with you!"

"And you just let him go?"

"Of course I did. He needed a piss and he was with you!"

"He wasn't with me!"

"We'll have to go back for him!"

"We'll never find him!"

"Well, we can't leave him!"

"What are we going to do?" Dave chipped in. "Search every pub in Sheffield? Tonight? Really?"

Dave saw the futility of the situation, but would not give up.

"We can't just leave him!"

"His missus will kill us."

Me and Sarah could only watch.

As the argument raged, I noticed that the railway-siding was swarming with policemen and most City fans had already left.

"Is this your van?" someone yelled just inches behind me.

Gary and the lads all spun round. "Yes!"

"Then get in it and fuck off back to Coventry now!" The police officer wasn't prepared to negotiate despite the dilemma that we found ourselves in, but Dave had to try.

"We're waiting for one of the lads, an old guy actually," Dave told him, "he got separated from us."

"Get in the van and piss off now or you're all nicked!" the officer roared. "Your choice!"

With heavy-hearts, we clambered into the van and headed home. For a long time Dave was silent in the driver's seat. They'd occasionally pipe up with a strategy for dealing with Gerry's missus, 'We'll tell her he was with us till we got back to The Pilot, but we ain't seen him since,' or 'He met up with his cousin from Cork'. Everyone nodded and said what great ideas they were, except Keith, who told Dave that Gerry was a grown man who could look after himself and that Dave shouldn't blame himself and should enjoy what had been a great day. Dave knew he was right, but chose not to say so.

Sarah fretted about Gerry all the way home. "I do hope he's OK," she whispered. "What if something happens?"

"He'll be fine," I assured her. "In fact he'll have the time of his life. A bloke like Gerry'll be alright, you'll see,"

The lads in the back grew rowdier as the journey went on and the last of the warm Tennents cans were supped.

We spoke about the semi-finals. Who would we draw? Where would we play? We had heard none of the other results as the van had no radio, but it didn't really matter to me. I was going to watch Coventry in an FA Cup semi-final, hopefully with the girl who was lying in my arms, and I could not have been happier.

< < < <   > > > >

When the lads dropped us back in town, we bid farewell to our rescuers, promising a trip to The Pilot to show our appreciation (and to find out what happened to Gerry)

And so me and Sarah found ourselves back in Coventry, and the deepest despair of that morning seemed like a long time ago. I felt like Dorothy arriving back in Kansas after surviving a tornado and seeing the Wizard of Oz.

Sarah was thinking the same thing. "Remember when we were outside that pub this morning?"

"I do," I nodded. "We nearly missed it!"

"I know."

"Did you have a good day out?" I asked.

"I did," she said. Her smile was huge and beautiful.

I wanted to kiss her again, but things seemed like they might be different now, like we'd shared a holiday romance and we were going back to our lives. Only, I didn't want to go back to my life without her.

Sarah took the decision out of my hands. She popped a kiss on my lips, only a peck, but it filled me with a promise of more of them to come.

<< < < >> > >

"I'm hungry," she said. "Do you want to come back to my house for dinner?"

"I- " Of course, I did. I wanted to spend as much time with her as I could, but-

"I can bring my friends back to dinner. It's not a crime," she smiled.

"Oh yeah," I said, "I forgot. I'm your college project. Right?"

"University project, to be precise. It has to be that way, for now," she said. "I hope that's OK?"

"I can do that."

We started walking. Side by side, but with a distance between us.

"Steve, you'll have to be patient with me," she said, both of us looking forward, "I'm sorry, but-"

"Don't be," I said, "I understand. Everything is going to be fine, you'll see."

She nodded, but didn't seem so certain as I was pretending to be.

"Oh," I said, "by the way, for appearance's sake, did we go to a football match today?"

Sarah smiled at me. "Yes, I do believe we did."

We walked a while, Sarah eyeing the people who passed us.

Maybe a minute went by, then she asked, "How come you don't live with your mum?"

"My mum moved to Bedworth, after my dad died, and I wanted to stay in Cov," I explained. "She lives with her boyfriend now, not that he's the reason I didn't want to move in, he's fine actually, a decent bloke."

Sarah looked a bit dazed by the conversation, her face so sadly serious.

I needed her to smile again.

I asked her, "Did you have fun today?"

And there it was, that smile.

Oh my God, I thought. Oh. My. God.

"Aren't you the video guy?" Sarah's dad asked.

"He is," Sarah jumped in. "We've been to a football match."

She sounded casual, convincing, but I could tell she wasn't used to lying to her dad.

She had introduced me to her parents in the kitchen. "I'm Ray," her dad said, "This is my wife Melissa."

She looked from me to Sarah, her mascara-lined eyes burning with questions, but her tiny lips remained frozen in place. Her hair was an auburn shade, long and straight, with a fringe that framed her face with three straight sides. She was beautiful, waif-like thin. I could see where Sarah got her looks from. Her mother was elegant, striking, but extremely cold, at least to me.

"Nice to meet you again, Mr Morales," I said. "Mrs Morales."

He nodded.

She left the room.

He looked mildly annoyed at me and for a moment there was an atmosphere.

"I'm helping Steve streamline his business," Sarah said.

"Oh, that's good," her dad said, "putting your Commerce skills to good use."

I over-smiled and said, "Aren't commas those curly full stops?"

Sarah smirked, and her dad didn't even flinch.

Too early, I told myself.

"Would you like to stay for dinner, Steven?" he asked me. "I'm going out for pizza."

"I'd love to," I said.

"I already asked him, dad," Sarah said and sat on the opposite side of the table.

She gave me a look that said both 'sorry' and 'no more jokes!' and I nearly laughed out loud.

Instead, I said to her, "What were you saying about how I reinvest my profits? That's a significant amount of money and I'm not sure even my market-share can deliver the yield I'm pushing for. I still think we should have a serious conversation about diversifying."

Behind her father's back, Sarah stuck her tongue out at me.

He had a wine bottle in his hand, reading the label.

Then he turned to me and said, "Be careful when diversifying, no two markets are ever the same."

"Daddy," Sarah said, her cool slowly fading, "we're talking."

"I've done my due diligence, sir," I said, looking closely at Sarah as she squirmed in her seat. "Research and customer testing. It'll need a lot of hard work but I know I can win the market's affection and retaining customer loyalty is my unique selling point. And the most important factor is my insatiable desire to be successful. Nothing else matters to me and nothing's going to get in my way."

Her dad had turned, listening to my waffle, and give me an appreciative nod. "You seem to know what you're doing-"

"Dad! Do you mind?"

He faked to leave with a gracious wave to Sarah, but then whispered to me, "What are you going into?"

"Computer games," I said. "It's gonna be huge."

He frowned but didn't reply.

"Anything from escaping from dungeons to building a city or surviving an earthquake, we'll have a game for it. Everybody's gonna be playing computer games soon."

"You think so?"

"I know so," I said, then looked up at him. "Don't you go stealing my idea!"

"It is a good idea," he said.

Sarah got up and pushed her dad out of the kitchen.

"Nice performance," she whispered.

"Do you think I overdid it?" I whispered back. "Or should I have played cute but dumb?"

"No, you did fine," she said but rolled her eyes, "especially the 'computer games thing."

"I think we fooled him," I whispered back. "Not bad for a ghetto-rat."

She kicked me under the table. "Don't overdo it at dinner."

"Are you doing anything on Tuesday night?" I asked.

"Tuesday?" she said, "What's wrong with Monday?"

"I didn't want to seem desperate."

Our voices were low, whispers and murmurs that we hoped were unintelligible to anyone outside the room.

"What did you have in mind?" she asked.

"I thought we could go for a curry and then a movie."

She considered it and nodded. No doubt she had just concocted a plausible cover-story. "Can you meet me outside the Lanch?"

I nodded and smiled. "Yes I can," then added, "Actually, I don't care if you think I'm desperate. Could we go on Monday?"

She laughed, "Monday it is."

We sat, enjoying the quiet and there being no need to talk. It was nice, but it didn't last.

The front door slammed and the house burst to life with voices and echoes and footsteps and more doors slamming.

"We're back!"

"When's dinner ready?"

"What are we having?"

I'd been pre-warned. Eldest sister Danielle was the Prom Queen, which coming from Sarah I took as a serious compliment. Her younger sister Candice was "a princess" and all three sisters helplessly spoiled Jordan, the youngest and the only boy. There were exactly two years between all the siblings, 'almost to the day', which made Daniella twenty, Candice sixteen and Jordan fourteen.

She had said before, 'My dad managed our family-planning on a tight schedule.'

"Where's Sarah?" one of the sister's yelled from the dining room.

"In here Candy," Sarah yelled back.

The door flew open and Candice slumped into the kitchen. "I dumped Andrew," she proclaimed.

She was a perfect replica of a younger Sarah, but her hair was straight and she wore too much make-up for a girl so young. The two sisters shared the same style; the expensive trainers and designer jeans, but Candice added jewellery. She wore gold necklaces, ear-rings and bracelets.

Sarah got up and hugged her sister. "Oh my God, Candy. Are you OK?"

She nodded and sniffed hard with a 'there'll be no tears' kind of determination.

"What did he do?" Sarah asked.

When Danielle appeared in the doorway, my immediate sympathy went to Mr Morales. As the father of the three Morales sisters, he must have had years of sleepless nights worrying about his beautiful daughters. She had taken the family movie-star genes to Oscar Winning levels. And she knew it.

"He booked a holiday with his mates! Can you believe it?" she explained.

Sarah leaned back from hugging Candice and asked her the question, "He booked a holiday? Without you?"

She nodded, her top lip pushed up to her button nose, and for a second the tears were about to burst into a torrent of heartbreak, but she held on and composed herself.

I didn't totally understand the connection between this apparently heinous crime and the resulting banishment, but I was living in a different world here, so I was happy to go with the flow.

In fact, I was making notes.

They seemed to be able to look after themselves, however, particularly under the guidance of Danielle, who exerted as much strength and power as she did pure attraction.

"I told her," she said, "nobody gets to treat you like that. Nobody in the world. And tell him there's no way he's gonna crawl back into your life, no matter what."

Candice had spotted me. She was staring at me over Sarah's shoulder and as the guest. I didn't think it was my place to talk first, so I smiled and waited.

Eventually, she spoke, her voice loaded with suspicion, "Who are you?"

I got the distinct impression that my worn out trainers and stone-washed-and-then-some jeans marked me as an outsider.

"I'm Steve," I said.

"What are you doing here?" Candice asked, her follow-up question no warmer than the first.

Danielle almost purred with sarcasm, "Yeah, what are you doing here?"

I said nothing and let Sarah rescue me.

"Steve's a friend of mine," she said, "We went to the football match today."

No doubt attracted by the voices, Jordan appeared beside Danielle. He was almost as tall as her, even with her heels, and he was munching on a take-away chicken leg.

Theatrically astounded, he asked Sarah, "You went to the football match?"

"Yes," she said.

"You went to the Coventry game? And you didn't even ask me!"

"Why would I ask you?" Sarah said.

"You knew I wanted to go!" he shouted at her.

Sarah rolled her eyes. "Jordan, you support Aston Villa anyway."

"Not anymore, I don't!"

I decided I didn't like Jordan.

< < < <   > > > >

When their mother calls that dinner is ready, Candice and Jordan dutifully head to the dining room.

Danielle remained in the doorway, and asked me, "So, did you enjoy the game?"

Her slight glance to her younger sister made it more than clear that she was not referring to the exploits of the mighty Sky Blues.

"I did," I told her. "I didn't think we had a chance, but here we are."

"Yep," she echoed, "Here you are."

Sarah hissed at her sister, "We're just friends!"

Danielle nodded, "I can see that."

"And it's been a pleasure to meet your family, Sarah," I said, "and honestly, I love how you all look out for each other. I respect that, and it's something you don't see often enough. There's nothing more important than looking out for your family."

<< << >> >>

There was another kiss, outside as I left. It was about eleven o'clock and, although I say it myself, I had done a sterling job of winning her family around. Me and Danielle were bosom-buddies, bonding over being the oldest sibling and our love of Madonna and Bon Jovi, although I had to fake some of the love. Even her mother had warmed a bit once she realised I would not tie them up and rob them. I played on the 'poor-kid trying to come good' angle without giving too many specifics, but stressing the disadvantages I'd have to overcome and the temptations I'd avoided to get where I am today (business-owner and all-round good guy).

The only problem was Jordan, who guilt-tripped Sarah about her not taking him to the match.

"Jordan," her dad said, "We'll go to the next game, how's that? What is it, Steven? The semi-final?"

"Well, there's a few League games before then-"

"Not the League games," he said and gave me a dismissive wave, "not interested in those, they're a waste of time, I mean the FA Cup game."

"Well," I said, rolling my lips together as deliberated how to answer. "The semi-final is in April. To get a ticket, you'll probably need to go to the League games and keep the ticket stub. It's how the club rewards the loyal fans."

Meaning, not you, I added in my head.

"So we'll buy the tickets, so what?"

I took a big bite of pizza to buy some time. For many years, I had hated this kind of thing where money is used to keep those less well off from getting tickets to big games. Sarah's dad was willing to pay for tickets to matches he had no intention of going to, just to qualify for tickets for the glamour game. I knew this happened all the time, but I never thought it would happen to Coventry.

I finished my pizza and explained, "You may also need a ticket from today's game."

Jordan pointed his fork at Sarah and shouted, "The one you went to without me!"

I was fairly sure that this spoilt little shit would get a slap, maybe two, but they all carried on as if nothing had happened.

Her dad sat back and looked at me for a few seconds before speaking. I met his stare and waited.

"Steven," he said, "I thought more of you, I'm disappointed because I thought you could get things done, take action, find a way to succeed, but all I'm hearing is excuses about tickets I need to buy and tickets I don't have. If it's too much for you, then-"

"It's not too much," I said, "It's just going to take a lot of work on my part, I'm sure you'll appreciate that."

"I'll appreciate it if you get two tickets," he said.

"I'll arrange it so you can kick-off, if you want."

He chuckled, perhaps a little too much. He seemed pleased with himself that he had got a response from me so easily.

I glanced at Sarah. She was looking down at her plate.

"I'll get you two tickets," I said, "no problem whatsoever."

"You're a clever guy. You've got connections, right? You'll sort it out," he said. And that seemed to be that.

For the rest of the meal, Candice lamented about what could've been with Andrew. Her mother debated holiday destinations. Her father asked me about the Computer Games idea again, but thankfully her mother cut him off 'No business at the table Ray' which appeared to be a house-rule, and Jordan mentioned three or four times how much easier his life would-be if he had a motorbike.

And I had spent all of my time watching Sarah, catching her eye, making her smile and wondering how I could continue what had happened today for the rest of my life.

CHAPTER TEN

Monday 16th March 1987

After I made a fair go of cleaning the bedsit, I headed into town for a bite and a trip round the market to pick up the Levi's money from Molly.

"Could you get me any Coventry flags or scarves?" she asked me.

The market, like the rest of the City, was in the grip of Cup fever with Sky Blue merchandise cropping up everywhere.

"I'll see what I can do."

She smiled and we hugged.

I should've done something before. I'd been caught up in the excitement and I hadn't thought of the opportunity, but there was now a new market. Everyone in Coventry was going to want or need a Coventry City flag, scarf, hat, rosette, framed photo, lunch box or anything else that could be produced quick and cheap.

Before going to meet Sarah at The Lanch, I took a detour to Foleshill Road to Bal's dad's textile factory.

Mr Sharma was a hard-working business-owner. He ensured that his factory served his community as much as it served itself, and he had a strong reputation as a firm but fair employer. He lived and breathed his work and thought anything else was a frivolous waste of time, the most frivolous and the most wasteful being following a football team.

I also knew that, frivolous or not, he would have seen the possibility of turning the Sky Blues into profit before most people had got out of bed.

"My order books are full, Steven," he interrupted me as soon as I raised the subject.

We were taking the opportunity to 'walk the floor' as we talked. Although he said he could only spare me five minutes, there was no reason we should waste those five minutes with just talking. Already about half of his products were football-related, mostly tri-colour flags on sticks, but also T-shirts and flat caps, all emblazoned with the Coventry City badge in cheap ink.

"I appreciate that, Mr Sharma, and I would expect no less. That's why I'm asking for just a small batch of items to offset the new economy faced by the market traders. They're struggling without merchandise and can't compete with these fly-by-night carpet-baggers who've moved in like parasites with their tacky knock-off FA Cup exploitation."

I wasn't exactly sure what carpet-baggers were, but I doubted if Mr Sharma did too.

"I produce my products under license Steven, I have signed contracts for exclusivity," he explained.

"But we both know that some things are more important than contracts and licenses. People, communities, the city of Coventry, is more important than Coventry City, never mind those who seek to profit from them! The market is under threat, I can see stalls closing if they can't make ends meet, and when these new traders have made their money, they'll be going back to Liverpool, Manchester or London, and Coventry will be even worse off now than we were before."

Mr Sharma stopped and picked out a sky blue rosette from the workbench tub. It looked so delicate and flimsy that I thought it might fall apart in his hands, but, after studying it for a few seconds, he laid it back in the tub, undamaged.

"Be here tomorrow, nine o'clock. I'll prepare a selection of items," he said.

"Thank you so much. You have saved Coventry market. They will be forever in your debt."

"And so will you," he said, "fifty quid, cash on delivery."

< < < <   > > > >

When I'd met Sarah coming out of the Lanch she smiled, but her body language said to stay at arm's length and I did as her body told me.

"It's Leeds!" I said.

"What is?"

"The cup draw, this morning. We've got Leeds United."

"Oh yes," she said. "All the boys were talking about it. I told them I went to the game on Saturday and they didn't believe me."

We wandered across town as I explained the reasons for the semi-final match to be played at a neutral ground and that it was yet to be announced.

Once she started nodding without talking, I guessed we'd probably covered all the discussion points about the football. I retrieved the Theatre One film-listings advert I had ripped out of the paper and debated over The Color of Money and Stand By Me, and I was careful not to declare a preference and handed the decision-making over to her.

She chose The Color of Money with the two-word explanation: 'Tom Cruise'. I was happy with that, but was more looking forward to seeing Paul Newman in the thirty-years sequel to The Hustler, which Sarah had never seen.

We discussed this as we turned the corner at the steps of Theatre One and a sharp left turn into the alley that lead to the back of the Taj Mahal, and my bedsit. My plan was to persuade Sarah to agree to try a curry and then the VIP treatment courtesy of Mr Chandra.

"This is a brave thing you're doing," I told Sarah as I put the key in the door.

She grabbed my arm, moved closer to me and whispered, "What is that smell?" She wrinkled her nose in disapproval.

"That is the curry restaurant downstairs," I said.

"Don't tell me!" she gasped. "It's not is it?"

"What?"

"It's the Taj Mahal, isn't it? No wonder you promised to take me there. You probably own it or something."

"I don't own it, I just rent this room from the man who does. Excuse the state of the place."

"Oh," she said, "How bad is it?"

"It hasn't had a woman's touch for a long time," I said. "A bit like me."

She raised an eyebrow. "Is that so?"

If Sarah had a strong first impression of my room, good or bad, then she hid it well. She had a casual look around the living room/kitchen/bedroom. Admittedly, there was a lot of clutter as I lacked storage space for the clothes, videotapes and assorted boom-boxes and video recorders that I hadn't been able to hide away. The good news was that the sofa and armchair were both clear and cleaned.

"Tea? Coffee?" I asked her.

She slipped off her Adidas jacket and, realising that I didn't have a coat stand, I draped it carefully over a tall chair in the kitchen.

"Coffee please," she said, "milk, no sugar."

"I just want to watch Midlands Today if that's OK. They've got the goals from the game and Jimmy Greaves has some humble-pie to eat."

I explained that since he had predicted us to lose every game since Stoke, Mr Greaves' had become our lucky charm. If he says we'll lose, then we're as good as through.

She dropped onto the sofa, picking a spot to the far left. I flipped on the TV. Blue Peter was on BBC1. I left it on and sat on the right.

"Jordan hasn't stopped talking about the semi-final," she said. "He hasn't stopped telling everyone that he's going."

"I haven't got the tickets yet," I said. I still didn't have a plan to get them either, but her family didn't seem too interested in those minor details.

She looked up in surprise. "You will though, won't you?"

"It's going to be difficult. They're going to be like gold-dust."

"But I thought you'd be able to buy them when you bought ours?"

"I can get ours," I said. "We have the stubs from the Wednesday game."

"I still don't understand how it works," she sighed.

I explained, "To make it fair, they restrict everyone to one ticket each-"

"I'm sure dad won't mind paying whatever it costs. It's for Jordan so, you know."

I shook my head. "OK, look, I'll do all I can, but you have to let him know there's no guarantee."

She nodded again, "I'll tell him."

As I settled down to see what Mr Greaves had to say for himself, Sarah took herself to my breakfast table and to 'do some work'. She took a brochure from her bag and became engrossed in it immediately.

I must admit I was intrigued, and when she asked me if she could use the loo, after I'd escorted her to the 'bathroom', I snuck back to take a peek. The brochure looked like a business proposal for a company called 'Helping Hands'.

When I heard the toilet being flushed, I placed the brochure back on the table.

"I hope it wasn't too industrial," I said of the facilities.

She smirked, "It was OK, but I couldn't find the concierge."

I shook my head. "He's useless. Consider him sacked."

She did, at least, seem comfortable and was soon back at the table, working on the brochure.

I tried to concentrate on the TV, but I was dying to find out more about what she was doing.

"Uni work?" I asked.

She looked up, startled, "What?"

I nodded at the brochure, "You're doing uni work?"

She looked at the brochure, confused, then said, "Yeah."

"What is it?" I asked.

"It's a business proposal. I'm assessing its potential."

"Interesting."

She nodded, but didn't bite.

I couldn't make my curiosity any more obvious, so I got up and sauntered over to the table.

She closed the brochure under the pretense of showing me the cover, but clearly she didn't want me to see the contents. She was terrible at hiding things.

Beneath the name of the company, 'Helping Hands', was a logo, a silhouette of two hands shaking and a slogan 'Social Justice in Action'.

"Looks like a charity organisation."

"It's a 'not-for-profit' business."

"Not for profit?" I asked, "Whats the point of that?"

She was staring at the cover, which she was obviously already familiar with, but it held her attention all the same.

"The idea is that a business exists to serve the community, to help those who need it rebuild their lives through their own contribution to business or productivity."

"Like a chain-gang?" I said.

She looked up at me, unhappy and finding no humour in my bad joke.

It was a bit out of order to take the piss out of this idea, but she'd got my back up a bit by trying to hide it from me.

"Well, it's not the best idea in the world, is it? How would it ever work?" I said.

"It doesn't matter," she said, and put the brochure back in her bag.

"You've got to assess its potential, right? So what do you think? It's a nice idea for a university student to dream up, but the real world doesn't work like that."

"It's about social justice. The fact that the 'real world' doesn't work like that is kind of the point. It's trying to demonstrate how profit can be traded for fairness in society. A company that employs the unemployed and has no need to reward its owners and investors is a flagship for social justice."

I shook my head. "Students wanting to change the world. If they want to understand what the under-privileged they should ask them what they want, not play games in a university class-room."

She got up and went to the sofa. Even though she looked quite cute when she was sulking, I realised I'd gone too far.

"Sarah, I was joking," I said. "You do know that, right?"

"Didn't you want to watch this?" she said, not looking away from the TV.

Jimmy Greaves was on, all smiles.

I took my seat beside her and put my arm around her. She didn't move.

When the big moment came, Greavesie predicted we'd lose.

"Yes! You beauty!"

"By the way," I said, "does your dad know about us?"

I smiled, trying to soften the blow of the intrusive question, but her eyes darted around the room like a rabbit looking for a burrow to bolt to.

"Does he know?" she said.

"Yeah."

"How would he know?"

"Well, like, if you told him."

She shook her head. "No, I haven't told him. Is that a problem?"

"No," I shrugged, "I just wondered if he knew about us or if you were still my business advisor."

"Are you upset?"

"No," I smiled and let out a little chuckle, "I just wanted to know for when we go to the game, but it's not a big deal."

"It's complicated, Steve," she said, drawing a sharp breath in. "You're going to have to trust me because I can't sort it out yet. I just can't."

I'd upset her, which wasn't what I meant to do. "I know, I know, it's OK," I said, gently squeezed my arm around and she put her head on my shoulder.

"I am sorry."

"It's my fault," I said, "I shouldn't have been so stupid."

Which may or may not have been true, but I supposed it was more complicated than I first thought. I just hoped it wasn't emotionally complicated on her part, because it wasn't on mine. But who knew?

Sarah got up and paced around the room.

She picked up the only framed photo I had. It was a holiday photo of me and my dad in Devon. I was about eight at the time and we were on a beach. She asked who he was, although there was a strong resemblance between me and him.

She brought the photo back to the sofa and stared at it.

"Do you mind talking about your dad?" she said.

"No, I like to talk about him," I said, "but it gets weird for the other person."

"You were twelve when he died?"

I nodded. "I have so many great memories of him, and I know a lot of people at the market who worked with him, so I get to hear a lot of stories about him too."

"Sounds like you're a chip off the old block, huh?"

Sarah put her hand on my arm. She looked too sad to speak.

"My dad was sixteen years older than I am now-"

"When he was thirty-five," Sarah said, finishing my sentence for me.

"I know-"

"So I've probably got sixteen years-"

"Is it-" she interrupted.

"Hereditary? They say it's not, but how would they really know? It might just be fate," I said and smiled. "Is there such a thing as hereditary fate?"

I was aware this wasn't strictly true, but didn't want to go into details.

Sarah slipped across the sofa and cuddled into me, her head on my chest.

"You don't really think so, do you?"

I did. In my head this was true, and as inevitable as day follows night.

But I didn't say that.

What I'd said wasn't a lie, it just hid some of the truth, "Maybe."

"But they said it wasn't hereditary."

"They said it's not, but then they say if it is they can treat it." I lied this time. "So I get checked now and again, because you never know, right?"

"So you shouldn't think you've only got until a certain age," she said.

"Well, I'm kind of used to thinking that way now. And why not?" I tried to sound as calm and sane as I could. "I want to live a lifetime before I'm thirty-five. After that, every day is a bonus."

Sarah just stared at the photo.

CHAPTER ELEVEN

Monday 23rd March 1987

That Monday morning, all over the city, people had started decorating their houses, hanging flags and banners and Sky Blue ribbons. Cars had City scarves streaming out of the back window or stretched across the parcel shelf. Shops also displayed their allegiances to the City with messages and banners of their own.

The club had announced that anyone who went to the home game against Oxford would be guaranteed a semi-final ticket. This was possible because our allocation for Hillsborough was 29,000 and Highfield Road held 27,000. Fans were reminded to keep their ticket stubs, and the gate was nearly 24,000.

I'd decided not to bother telling Sarah to remind her dad that he needed tickets to the game, and Sarah hadn't mentioned it, so I hoped that they had changed their plans. Spending a day with her dad and Jordan wasn't exactly how I planned to enjoy the biggest game of my life. It would be far better if just me and Sarah alone.

I took Sarah to the Oxford game, which was on a Friday night, and we stood on the kop beneath the scoreboard. Her wonder and enthusiasm captivated me entirely. She wanted to know everything about the ground and the club and I just wanted to look into her eyes as she asked the questions. We won three-nil, all the goals being scored at the West End, the first an amazing 'Dave Bennett Special' where he danced past two defenders and hit the far top corner from an impossible angle.

My hands were trembling as I tucked them in my wallet and my mind struggled to comprehend the fact that I was going to buy tickets for an FA Cup semi-final tie involving Coventry City.

I got down to Highfield Road at seven o'clock and there was already a queue that spread down Thackhall Street.

I joined the back of the line and got chatting with the guys around me.

"Looks like I'm gonna be late for work," said one, "but I'm picking up the bosses ticket too, so I'm holding it for ransom, in case I get sacked."

Everyone was all-smiles. Spirits were sky high, which was only to be expected. Everyone was talking about it. The 'Feel-Good Factor' was everywhere and the Coventry Evening Telegraph even reported that productivity was up in many of the city's factories.

"I had to phone in sick," said the older guy behind us, "they can sack me, but I'm not missing this match."

At eight-thirty the doors opened and by nine o'clock I had in my hand two FA Cup semi-final tickets. I paused at the door to study them. They were a white, pink and light green colour, no actual pictures or graphics on them, just a light watermark.

I made sure they were both safely in my wallet and headed home to place my treasured tickets in a safe place.

The game itself had moved, on the advice of the South Yorkshire Police, from the traditional Saturday to an early kick-off on the Sunday. They did this because of the 'reputation' of the Leeds fans. The plan was to stop them going to the pub for three hours before the match. Whether this made any difference, I was never sure. If people want to drink, in my experience, then they will.

CHAPTER TWELVE

Saturday 4th April 1987

So, on the spur of the moment, I headed to Nottingham.

But, take it from me, spending a Saturday afternoon on the terrace at the City Ground watching Cov play out a nil-nil draw with Nottingham Forest wasn't as exciting as it sounds. I went with Andy, Chris and Bal on the coach and although there was a big contingent of Cov fans making a lot of noise, it didn't translate across the pitch to the players on either side.

Or maybe I just wasn't in the mood. The previous Saturday we'd been to Villa again, to see us lose again. Although Villa were bottom of the league, it was no consolation to us as their fans poured scorn on us from the stand above the away enclosure.

Out of principal me and Chris always stayed on the terrace after the final whistle to goad the Villa fans in the stand above the away end. They would then pelt us with missiles, many of which were coins.

The four foot high wall at the back of the terrace provided us with enough cover to crouch behind and then, during a lull in the barrage, we'd dash out and grab as many coins as we could. This collection phase would double-up as the next goading phase, as once we were spotted, the shelling would begin again and we would scramble back to the safety of the wall. It usually took three or four cycles of the process and we would collect our ticket money in small change.

"Imagine if we ever won! We'd be rich!" Chris joked. However, that had never happened, so who knows?

However, where Villa was an annual event, going to Forrest was more of a diversion.

Sarah had declared herself unavailable that night as she had a 'family-thing' on, not that she'd lie, but it was one of those times where there was no substance to it and no detail. I wasn't being given the full story. But, like always, I didn't push the matter. I was devising a little plan of my own. Seeing that she was worried about telling her dad that we were 'more than friends', to the point that was becoming embarrassing for me, I thought I'd tell him myself, let the big fat cat right out of the big fat bag. Like ripping off a plaster, it might sting for a second, but soon everyone would get over it. I just had to pick my moment and my words carefully.

I'd also not mentioned to them that they needed tickets for the Oxford game of a few weeks ago, and that boat had now sailed, so to speak.

I thought more about my dilemma than I did about the game that was being played out before me.

Another City attack broke down once we crossed the halfway line and both sides gave the ball away in a demonstration of poor control and even worse passing.

My mind started to role-play certain scenarios where I could leave the rich, successful and highly protective Mr Morales, in no doubt that I was doing more with his daughter than taking her business advice.

"I'm going to get another pie. Do you want one?"

With my internal plotting and general level of a thousand conversations in the Cov end, I didn't take in what was being said.

A hard shove in the back made me pay more attention. "Oi! Deaf-head!" Chris shouted, "What's up with you tonight?"

I gave him a little shove back to let him know I was a bit narked, then shrugged, "Nothing's wrong with me."

"Yeah, right," Andy said, "You've got a face like a slapped arse, and you were the same at Villa."

"That's because we lost-"

"Bullshit! You were mardy before we even got there," Andy sneered.

Bal looked at me without speaking and his disappointed expression was deeper than any of their insults.

It was true; I had been a bit stroppy, and I needed to snap out of it.

"So, do you want a pie or not?" Chris asked.

"Yeah," I said, "I'll come with you. We're not going to miss anything here."

We got to the pie-man, a large rotund kind of guy who clearly enjoyed consuming his product but had less enthusiasm for the customer-facing aspect of it.

"Only steak and kidney left," he declared as we approached.

"Four please," Chris replied.

"Four pounds," said the pie-man.

"A pound each?" Chris roared. "Are you having a laugh?"

The pie-man did a fairly good Chris-impression with a retort of, "Are you having a pie?"

Chris didn't speak and didn't move.

"You can always try your luck at any of our competitors' outlets," the pie-man sneered. "Oh wait! There aren't any!"

Unsurprisingly, Chris bought the pies, and the game ended 0-0.

"So are you and this girl getting serious?" Chris asked.

"Which girl?" I said. It wasn't like he didn't know her name, he just didn't like saying it for some reason.

He shrugged. He still wasn't going to say it.

"Yeah, I'm fairly serious."

"Where's she from again?" he asks.

"Kenilworth Road."

Chris shakes his head. "I mean where is she from, not where does she live."

"I don't know," I said, "Guatemala, I think. Is it important?"

Chris shook his head. "Probably not," he said, "unless she decides to go back there or something."

"I don't think-"

"Where is Guatemala anyway?"

"I don't know," I said. "And she might decide to go back there, or she might decide she's going to be a nun, or she might decide that all my friends are dickheads, or she might decide to do a lot of things, but what's your point?"

"I'm just saying," Chris said, "that you're going nuts over this girl and you don't know if she'll be around much longer. You know, don't lose perspective on this."

"Don't lose perspective?" I repeated. That was the most un-Chris-like thing he had ever said, which meant he heard that from someone else, probably Bal.

"I'm just saying-"

"How's Karen, by the way?" I said, "I haven't seen her in ages. Why don't you bring her to a match or a night out or something?"

"She doesn't like football," he said.

"She doesn't like football? She used to like it. What changed? Maybe she doesn't like being around us? Maybe she thinks she's better than us. She likes drinking but she won't come out with us? You should sort this out mate, have a word with her."

"What are you talking about?" Chris said.

I took a bite of my pie and looked at him as I chewed it.

"I'm talking about your girlfriend," I said, "and I'm telling you how to run your life."

Chris breathed out through his nose. "You know, with Karen and Sarah, it's not the same."

"I'm glad you remember her name," I said. "Just do me a favour and let me look after my love-life, if that's OK?"

Chris took a bite of his own pie and nodded.

"And say Hi to Karen for me," I said, "tell her I'll pop round soon and we can catch up."

We were both quiet for the rest of the game.

As we waited in the pen, kept in detention after class as always, talk turned to the conversation I had been hoping to avoid.

"How we getting to Hillsborough?" Bal asked.

All eyes turned to me, although the question was aimed at the group.

I said nothing, which kind of said it all.

"Have you booked onto the coach, Steve?" Bal asked.

They all knew the answer to the question, including Bal, but he couldn't stand the awkward silence, whereas Chris and Andy would suffer it, as long as I suffered more.

"I'm thinking of making a weekend of it," I said. "I'll meet up at the ground."

"Like you did in the quarters?" Chris said.

"On Hillsborough Spion Kop," Andy added, "with twenty thousand people?"

I shrugged. Not a big deal.

"I hope she's worth it," Chris said.

"Why don't you bring her with you?" Bal said, his voice sounded pleading. He wanted to fix his family of friends.

"Her brothers coming too," I said. "I'll meet you there. It's not a problem, is it?"

Chris sneered, and echoed, "It's not a problem, is it?"

"Biggest game in the history of the world and you're dumping us for a bird?" Andy said. "You need to have a word with yourself."

"I'm going to the game with my girlfriend. I'll meet you there if you want me to. That's what's going to happen," I said.

Chris gave me a stare, more disappointment, but I was building an immunity to disappointing stares, so I stared back. He was always likely to kick-off and the fact that we were good mates didn't mean he would make an exception.

We were the last to realise that the gates had opened and people were shuffling out. We'd continued this staring match, but to draw it to a conclusion, I slowly raised both eyebrows, which was me questioning whether Chris wanted to escalate or diffuse the conflict.

With a nod, he diffused the argument. And we bumped shoulders together as we turned to shuffle along with the crowd.

I told Andy that Sarah was the work-experience girl and that she'd be joining us on the video round for the night.

Everything went really well. We had one of our best takes ever and no problems with returns for once.

Sarah and Andy got on like a house on fire and were united in a joint-effort of taking the piss out of me.

She would tee him up with questions about what I was like at school and he would slam-dunk it with embarrassing tales of my academic career and extra-curricular activities.

As I made my way back to Sarah's house, the three of us on the bench seat, Andy spilt the last, and by no means the least, funny story of my past.

"He was particularly curious during sex-education," Andy told her. "The teacher, Miss Flowers, explained that before and during intercourse, the male would be 'aroused', then she explained exactly what she meant by arousal-"

"Oh my God, she had to describe arousal to pre-high school kids?" Sarah said. "The poor woman."

"Exactly," Andy went on, "and then she says 'any questions?'"

Here he paused for effect.

I shook my head. "I asked a perfectly legit question," I told them both.

"Only one person had his hand up," Andy said, "And the teacher goes, 'Yes, Steven?' and he says, 'What if he needs to pee, Miss?'"

Sarah laughed, "That was a fair question."

Andy nodded. "It was. But Miss Flowers went whiter than a nun's backside and tried to explain that it just wasn't possible. Only that's not enough for young Steven. His hand goes up again, and he says, 'What if he's bursting, Miss?'

"And she goes, 'I've answered that question already. Does anybody else have a different question?' And again there's only person with his hand up, but she's ignoring him, Then this girl called Karen puts her hand her up and Miss Flowers goes, 'Yes Karen?' and she says, 'I think Steven has a question Miss'."

Sarah was in a fit of giggles.

"And Miss Flowers goes, 'Steven-' and he goes, 'Right, he's absolutely bursting, yeah? He wants to go so bad that it hurts and there's some pee coming out already cos he can't hold it anymore. Are you telling me he can't go? Really?' and the class was in bits, it was hilarious,"

Sarah pulled a face amid her laughter. "There's some pee coming out?" she repeated, "Oh my God! That is so gross!"

"I still say it was a fair question," I said, deadpan. "When you gotta go, you gotta go, it's a law of nature."

CHAPTER THIRTEEN

Sunday 5th April 1987

I parked the van on my mum's driveway and took Sarah to the back door.

I'd never let myself in to mum's house before and as I reached for the door handle Sarah grabbed my wrist.

For a second, I thought she was backing out. She'd been a bag of nerves all morning and she looked scared to death.

"Do I look OK?" she asked.

I laughed. It seemed ridiculous that she could be concerned about how she looked. "You're asking me if you look OK?" I said to her, "When we both know that you look stunningly beautiful?"

"Please don't tease me," she whispered.

I kissed her lips and said, "You look great."

I kissed her again, then reached for the door handle.

"Get ready. Here we go!"

And I opened the door.

< < < <   > > > >

"I hope you enjoyed that, Sarah," my mum said,

Sarah had placed her knife beside the fork on her empty plate.

"Mrs McKenzie, thank you so much," she smiled. "It was a beautiful meal. Steve said you were an amazing chef and you absolutely are."

"Please call me Helen," mum told her, "and thank you. It's been our pleasure to have you here."

Sunday dinner had gone better than I could have dreamed of. Sarah and mum had hit it off and bonded instantly over their shared role as looking after me.

They'd covered family, fashion, beauty, Sarah's Uni, mum's business, 'men', money. They had covered all the big stuff without getting into the specifics.

It was great to listen to them talking, and I had even had an enjoyable chat with Derek, mostly about business.

"You can't be the boss and everyone's mate," he told me, "that's not going to work when the time comes to make tough decisions."

I nodded. That made sense.

"It can be a lonely place, but, if you're built a certain way, it's the only place you can be."

"I'm finding that out," I said.

"And once you've got things working the way you want," he said in a lower voice, "and you've got a little extra capital, my advice is to invest it. Put a little into shares and add to it when you can. It'll build up from there and that's your security in the leaner times, and there will be leaner times. Trust me, I learned the hard way."

<< < <   > > > >

I helped mum clear the plates away, an honour that was denied Derek and Sarah.

'No, I insist you sit down and let me and Steve clear up. Trifle?'

I must have had a million bowls of my mum's trifle in my lifetime and every one tastes better than the last.

Sarah savoured hers too, and I was convinced there was no way she could fake that level of pleasure.

Then my mum said to Sarah, "I hear Steve took you to the football."

Sarah nodded, "Yes, we went to Hillsborough, we played Sheffield Wednesday, and Coventry won three-one." After each point she made, she looked at me for confirmation, and I nodded approvingly.

"Well done," I said.

"And Dave Houchen scored twice," she went on.

"Keith Houchen," I corrected her.

She laughed. "I gave it my best shot. So many names to remember!"

"They did well," my mum said, "and now they're in the semi-finals."

"Yes, I wasn't really into football before, but the entire city has gone crazy about it. My brother wants to go so badly, he never stops talking about it, and he's never been to a game before."

"Oh, he'll love it," mum said.

Sarah nodded, "Steve is going to get him tickets," she said, then added, "Well, if he can."

And it was at that point that the whole day collapsed around my ears.

"I thought it was sold out," Derek said.

"I've got a few irons in a few fires," I said. "Something will come up. No problem."

Derek got to his feet and wiped his chin with his napkin. "Well, why didn't you say so?" he said. "Sarah, this is your lucky day! It just so happens that because my company sponsor the club, I've got spare tickets I was going to give away. I would be delighted to let you have them."

"Derek," I said, "you don't need to do that. Honestly, I've got it covered."

"It's no problem, Steve." Derek smiled as he circled the table. "I was considering going myself, but even if they win, we'll be missing the final because of the wedding, so I haven't let myself get too personally involved!"

And he was gone.

Sarah asked me, "Why didn't you say Derek could get tickets?"

I had no answer. Not one that I could give with my mother was sitting opposite me at least. I didn't even have to look up to know that she was watching me. She always knew when something was going down.

And then, as if this conundrum I found myself in couldn't get any worse, Sarah said, "It is such an unfortunate that the wedding and the Final are on the same day, isn't it? I mean all these years-"

"Yes, it is," I said, "It's very unfortunate."

"At the end of the day," my mum said, clearly reading my mind, "it's just one of those things, nothing we can do about it."

"Maybe you can tape it," Sarah suggested to me, "then you can watch it later."

"I don't want to talk about it," I said, staring at the table. "If we talk about it, we'll jinx it and they'll lose."

Sarah frowned, "I was just trying to help-"

"I know," I looked up and tried to smile at her and my mother, "but trust me, if we talk about the Final before we've won the Semi, then it will jinx it, so-"

And then Derek returned and placed two FA Cup Semi-Final tickets on the table between me and Sarah.

"There you go!" he said. "Enjoy!"

"You knew how much it meant to my brother," Sarah said.

We were back in the van, driving past the gas-works on the A444. She'd asked me why I hadn't asked Derek for the tickets.

"Sarah," I said, not sure how to best explain this, "I didn't want to be in his debt."

"What about Jordan? Didn't your promise to my brother mean anything? Or is it just about your family?"

"Jordan's never even been to a football match and now he's phoning Child-Line to report he's been neglected? Come on, Sarah, it would probably do him good not to get what he wants just for once."

"So you're saying he's spoilt too?"

I couldn't believe I was hearing this, but I didn't want to push the issue.

"Derek's my mum's boyfriend, and-"

"Your mum's boyfriend? What's that got to do with it?"

"I don't want to hurt my mum," I said. "Can't you see that?"

"No, I can't," she said. "Derek, kindly, wants to give you two tickets for my dad and Jordan: How is that going to hurt your mother?"

I realised I was driving too fast, but didn't want to slow down. I took a right and headed towards Holbrooks, hoping that taking a different route might somehow keep me engaged enough not to let this become a full-scale argument.

"Explain it to me, Steve," Sarah insisted.

"Because what Derek did for us was a very kind and generous thing," I said.

She gasped in exasperation and raised her arms in a question.

"So now I owe Derek a kindness in return," I said.

I glanced across at her and her face told me she now understood.

I carried on anyway, "So it will hurt my mother-"

"-when you don't go to the wedding," she completed my sentence.

"Yes."

"Steve, you can't go to a football match on your sister's wedding day," she said very slowly. "You just can't-"

"She's not my sister," I said.

"Step-sister then, my mistake!"

"I hardly know her, I've met her about five times."

"So just think about how much it will hurt your mum." she said.

"I haven't thought about much else," I told her.

And I had nothing else to add.

CHAPTER FOURTEEN

Sunday 12th April 1987

On the morning of the biggest game in our history, I was not in the best of moods.

My video round the night before had been a disaster. Andy had let me down at the last minute, and I decided to do it on my own. And that was asking for trouble, but at the time I didn't want to let people down.

When three grubby kids in Cheylesmore stole some movies from the van, I couldn't go after them and had to endure their taunts from the end of the street. At my next stop, I lost it with a female customer who didn't want to pay and I gave her a few choice words. When she relayed my comments to her two brothers, I had no choice but to make a sharp exit.

With three stops left and being well behind schedule, I called it a night, which meant I was letting people down after all. I had films out that hadn't been collected and was out of pocket with the stolen movies.

I knew I couldn't do the round on my own, but I couldn't rely on Andy to be doing me favours every Saturday night, and I couldn't afford anybody else.

There was nothing I could do about it that morning, so I tried to put it behind me, or at least out of my mind, for a few hours.

I was also in the dog-house with Sarah over Derek giving us the tickets for her dad and Jordan. She'd relayed me her dad's thanks, but then added that her dad wanted me to arrange transport. Was this some kind of punishment? Whose side was she on?

"Sarah," I said, trying to be diplomatic, "Your dad's got more cars than the Co-Op car park."

"He can't drive there," she said, "he doesn't know where it is."

"I can direct him," I said, "there's fifty thousand people going, we'll just follow them!"

"He doesn't want to drive, Steve," she said. End of.

I'd surrendered, as always, and managed to book a Toyota Space Cruiser from a Mini-Van hire firm near Cov airport.

We agreed to meet there at nine o'clock and I got there at eight-forty-five. I wanted everything to be ready to go when Sarah arrived with her family.

Except, weirdly, the car park was empty, not a Space Cruiser, or any kind of mini-van, in sight, which struck me as strange for a vehicle hire firm.

I stepped into the Porta-Cabin and my worst fears were confirmed.

"We're terribly sorry, but we've got a bit of a problem."

"What?"

The guy was skinny, wore glasses and a grey cow-gown with the firm's logo on the pocket. Very professional.

I hoped that this problem of which he spoke was marginal, trivial and a matter of professional pride to them, but of no particular consequence to me in the circumstances. However, the look on his face told me that this would not be the case.

Stood behind his desk in the freezing cold porta-cabin, he looked like a man with not only no van, but no Plan B. Or Plan C.

I knew immediately exactly what had happened, and that it was partly, if not completely, my fault.

"There's no vehicle, is there?" I said.

He shook his head.

"They were all booked out for yesterday, weren't they?"

He nodded.

"And they didn't return them, did they?"

He shook his head again.

Obviously, the Space Cruiser, and every other mini-bus this company hired out, had been booked for the original day of the game, yesterday. Once the game was switched to the Sunday bookings hadn't been cancelled or rescheduled. They had simply collected their vehicles and had kept them overnight and were now on their way to Sheffield.

"Maybe one will be returned soon," the man offered.

I shook my head. "I don't think so," I said. "Have you got anything? Any kind of vehicle?"

He pouted, as if pushing his lips out would aid his thought process, but apparently, it didn't, and, as a result, he shook his head. "No," he said. "Sorry."

"Great!" I sighed.

Before it really sank in that we were once again going to have to find an alternative form of transport to the game, Sarah's dad's Toyota MR2 rolled into the car park and glided to a halt.

I stepped out of the Portacabin to face this problem and put on a suitably grim expression in an attempt to fore-shadow the bad news.

Her dad and Jordan got out of the car, but there was no Sarah.

"Mr Morales," I said, "I'm afraid we have a problem."

I expect he had already suspected this may be the case, as there was not a single mini-bus in sight.

"What problem?" he said, forcing me to explain exactly what it was.

I said. "The Land Cruiser we booked hasn't been returned from yesterday."

"We booked?" he said. "Don't you mean 'you booked'?"

Jordan grinned

"We'll just have to drive up there," I said.

"Great!" Jordan shouted, throwing his arms up and kicking a loose pebble across the concrete.

Sarah's dad said, "This is a two-seater car." He cocked his thumb at the Toyota MR2. "It's not a problem, is it? As you say, you'll just have to drive up there. You did manage to get the tickets, didn't you?"

The tone of the question, compared to what I had gone through to get them, pissed me off more than anything he had said. I was sorely tempted to say 'No', but he already knew I had them and I was too down to argue.

I fished out my wallet and took out the tickets, but they stayed in my hand. "Where's Sarah?" I asked him.

"Sarah?" he frowned.

"Yes, Sarah," I said, "She's coming to the game with me."

"Really?" he smirked. "Are you sure about that?"

"I've been seeing her every day for-"

"She's not going to the game with you," he said, "Something's come up."

"What?"

"What do you think, Steve?" he said. "Have a wild guess."

"I don't know what you're talking about," I told him. "We've been seeing each other for-"

Her dad nudged Jordan and without taking his eyes off me, said, "Tell him what you told me in the car."

"What about?" Jordan said.

"What's Sarah doing today?"

"Oh yeah," Jordan nodded. "I heard her on the phone. She's meeting Greg."

Her dad smiled, all too triumphantly.

"Who's Greg?" I said.

And her dad laughed. "Greg's her boyfriend," he said.

I shook my head. I couldn't bring myself to say 'No', but-

"Oh!" her dad said, "Did you think-" He frowned, laying on the theatrics. "Did you think she was serious with you? Come on Steve, I thought you were smarter than that. Couldn't you see what was happening here?"

"I know exactly what's happening here," I said.

Her dad looked down and chuckled as he nodded at me to Jordan.

"Yeah sure, Steve. How much do I owe you for the tickets?" he said.

Jordan was grinning, trying to look menacing.

I looked his dad in the eye. He stared back at me.

I never hated anyone more in my life, but I hated more that I'd allowed myself to be manoeuvred into this position.

I handed him the two tickets.

"How much do I owe you?" he said again.

I put my hands in my pockets and shook my head.

"Nothing," I said, "I don't want your money."

"You've got a nerve!" he said at me, "You don't want my money? Well, we'll see about that."

"Yeah, we will," I shouted back. "Why would I ever want anything from you?"

"Oh yeah, well, you wanna know why Sarah's not here? What came up?" he was nearly spitting the words at me. "Her life came up. Her real life that you know nothing about and you can

never understand. Her future. It's like my American friends say Steve, 'Look at the big picture, and you'll see you're not in it'. That's why she's not here."

My only reaction was to shake my head. I wanted to tell him that I knew he was lying, but I knew that wasn't true.

"Did you really think that she was interested in you? Really? Oh my God, Steve! Come on!"

"Who do you think she's been with for the last two months?" I shouted at him and took a step forward. Jordan immediately stepped back and I shot him a stare that made him take another.

"You're a fool," he said, "You don't understand-"

"No," I said, "you don't understand. You think you have control over your family, but you don't. And you're gonna find that out real soon."

He started waving his finger at me.

"I don't want to see you anywhere near my house ever again," he said. I stepped forward again, tempting that finger to just brush my face and give me a reason to deck him. It poked and prodded the air just inches in front of my eyes. "And I don't want you anywhere near my daughter!"

"I know what you want, we'll see what you get."

I walked away. From behind me, I heard him tell Jordan to get in the car.

I sat in the movie-van until Sarah's dad and brother left.

I thought about phoning round the lads to get picked-up, but couldn't bring myself to do it.

I decided to drive up, but first I had to drop by Sarah's.

< < < <   > > > >

The M1 was an absolute nightmare. I got to Hillsborough at exactly twelve-forty. The game had started. I was sure they'd still let me in, but first I had to park. They allocated the City fans the enormous expanse of the Spion Kop. It seemed a strange decision as they had allocated Leeds more tickets and were in the smaller Leppings Lane end. This was so that they would segregate the fans outside the ground as well as in. Vehicles from Coventry would arrive from the east, by the M1, and Leeds from the West. A heavy police presence would ensure that no one crossed the dividing line across the streets around the ground.

In the make-shift car park beside the enormous stands of Hillsborough, which was basically a waste-ground that, over the years, had compacted mud as hard as concrete, I could see lines and lines of cars as far as the horizon. I still had to park and then walk all the way back, which could take another fifteen minutes. They'd be kicking off the second half by the time I got in.

A policeman flagged me down. He smiled politely and gave me a hand signal to wind the window down, so I did. He put his head through the window and glanced at the empty insides.

"Where's all ya' mates?" he said, "Did you leave 'em at t'service station?"

"No, it's just me, long story," I said, trying to convey my impatience without appearing getting his back up.

"Well, the game's been delayed by fifteen minutes because of crowd congestion," he said, "so they've been playing for about ten minutes."

"That's good," I said, "Can I go?"

"And your keeper," he said. "Oggovic, no, Ogro, no, Ogrizazovic."

"Steve Ogrizovic," I said. "What about him?"

"He's made, err..."

"He's made what? A mistake? Was there a penalty? Are we losing?"

"No, no, no. He's made a great save."

"OK, good thanks. Can I go now? Will they still let me in?"

"Have you got a ticket?"

"Yes!"

"Then you'll be fine. Away you go."

I thanked him and headed to the far reaches of the car park, knowing that I may be a lot of things today, but fine would not be one of them.

<< < < > > > >

As I jogged up to the stadium, I could follow the ebb and flow of the game by the roar of either set of fans. To my left were Leeds, sounding like ferocious warriors, and to my right were

Coventry, the expectant, hopeful twelfth man of the team. It sounded very much like Leeds were on top. I checked my watch. It was twelve forty-five.

I hadn't seen a soul outside the ground and was panicking about not being allowed in. I picked up my pace to a sprint, hit the steps to the turnstiles two at a time and as I was striding up, the roar hit me.

Leeds had scored.

I got into the ground and was immediately disorientated. We were at the opposite end to the Quarter Final and instead of facing the mass of 29,000 fans behind the goal, I was part of it. But it didn't feel real. I'd never missed a kick-off before and the game was twenty minutes old already. I had no history of what had happened and had to try to pick up the thread of how the game was going. The City fans around me were saying that we hadn't got into the game as yet and, if anything, Leeds looked like scoring again.

I made my way to the very front as there was more space there. I couldn't face the hustle and bustle of the elbow to elbow argy-bargy that I'd usually love.

Even as the next thirty minutes unfolded, I couldn't really recall anything that had happened. I wondered if I'd done the right thing, but that lead me to think about when I'd actually made that decision, which was outside Sarah's house, watching her get into her boyfriend's car. Greg's Audi Quattro.

It was almost by instinct alone that I'd sped away in the van and driven like a lunatic across town and headed north on the M69. I was running into the arms of Coventry City, who although they'd let me down many times, had never been guilty of treachery, just being shit sometimes. Or most of the time.

How could she do that? Was her dad right? Had she been playing me the whole time? And I had thought she was a terrible liar.

I asked myself all these questions for the two-hour journey, storming up the motorway in my van. I knew I should put her out of my mind, but that was easier said than done.

At one point, I was doing eighty in the middle lane, going over the disaster that the day had become, when I noticed that the traffic ahead had stopped dead. I knew in that instant that I could not avoid ploughing into the blue Vauxhall Cavalier forty yards in front of me. I hit the brakes with both feet, pulling the steering wheel back with both hands to apply even more foot pressure to the brake, but it was hopeless. I wasn't going to stop in time. Without thinking, I took a risk on the only chance I had to come out of this unscathed; I swerved blindly across the inside lane and then onto the hard shoulder.

I closed my eyes and the van shuddered to a halt. Car horns blared their disapproval, but I hadn't hit anything. I opened the van door and looked out at the now stationary lines of cars. None seemed to have collided, but plenty of drivers and passengers were quick to offer their angered opinions of my driving skills.

I managed to ignore them, although I agreed with their assessments, and I sought out the blue Cavalier. In the front were a mum and dad and there was two kids in the back. They were staring at me, all of their faces blank and emotionless. The alternative, which I'd only avoided by the skin of my teeth, gave me something else to think of instead of my tattered love-life.

I tried to concentrate on the match, but that gave me very little hope of the day getting better. It had been a pure disaster.

The team was wracked with nerves. Players normally confident on the ball were shirking their responsibility. Instead of looking for a probing pass, they'd play long balls that came to nothing or short balls that played their teammates into trouble. As a result, Leeds had their tails up and as they tore into us, we continued to make life difficult for ourselves. Even Benno seemed reluctant to go past a player and if it weren't for Oggy's saves and commanding the defence were definitely have been two-down.

Then, somehow, we steadied the ship, we started to play our own game and cause them a few problems.

Cyril got past his defender and into the box, but instead of pulling the trigger and hammering it past Mervyn Day, he shaped to shoot, then took another touch, and when the shot came the net remained frozen and the ball flew into the crowd.

Minutes later, Dave Bennett, who had found his feet and was now dancing past defenders, beat three in the box and bobbled the ball across the six-yard box and it evaded everyone to land at Cyril's feet. I leapt up, arms raised as Cyril would undoubtedly now rip the net from the posts, but again we were left wondering how had Big C missed?

But we were now back to our best.

We were going to score, I promised myself.

Twenty-thousand Cov fans agreed and a chorus of, "We're gonna score in a minute!" rang out.

The Leeds fans responded with a rendition of "Marching on together" followed by their warrior chant of, "Leeds! Leeds! Leeds!" Their support was the most passionate I'd seen in many a year, except for ours, but there was also an aggressive edge to it. Even the old ladies amongst them were scary.

And then we had a quick break down the right-wing and Dave Phillips flashed in a cross that Cyril met from what looked to me like a few yards out. Once he connected, I was certain that finally on the third attempt Cyril would be rewarded, but again somehow the ball flew wide.

I wasn't the only one who was thinking then that the football gods were against us, because there was no other explanation for the finest striker in English football to miss three opportunities in a matter of minutes. Fate was intervening in the cruelest of fashions and Coventry City were once again the victims. And if we needed any further proof, then it was provided just before half-time when Benno was once again tip-toeing through the defence and provided the ball to Houchen, who had scored three times in the Cup so far including one at Old Trafford and two on this ground. Houch took two touches to tee up his unchallenged shot, and again it sailed wide.

The evidence was obvious. If Keith Houchen can't score in an FA Cup tie, then it is definitely not your day.

Even so, we got behind the team. If there was a group of players who could overcome the gods, then it was this team. At half-time, we knew that George and John would perform a magic spell on each of them and the second half would be ours.

Fifteen minutes after the restart, and just ten yards in front of me, there was a turning point in the game. From midfield, we played the ball down the right channel, intended for Dave Bennett, but the Leeds defender, Brendan Ormsby, got there first and shepherded the ball out for a goal-kick. He watched

Bennett over his right shoulder and stepped across the ball to block Bennett, but somehow, Benno slid underneath the defender and scooped the ball out from his clutches.

The ball rolled obligingly on the line as both players went down and I feared Ormsby would grab Benno or there's be a tangle of legs, but Bennett was up and to the ball. As he looked up, he saw Lloyd McGrath unmarked in the six-yard box level with the near post. If Benno could thread the pass past two defenders, then Lloyd McGrath, whose goals were as rare as rocking horse shit, would put us right back in the game.

And thread the pass he did.

But the ball went behind McGrath and he missed it completely.

We howled, "Noooo!"

How was this even possible?

It was like a knife had been plunged into our hearts and was being viciously twisted.

The ball bounced once, twice, three times across the box and as if by magic, it landed at the feet of Mickey Gynn, who, just like he did at Stoke, planted the ball firmly into the bottom corner of the net and we erupted with joy as the football gods smiled down on their creation.

We had scored a goal, and it had never felt so good.

I was bouncing with energy, screaming and punching the air. It was a new world and anything was possible. Now that we had done it once, we could even score again! That feeling of living the dream, the fantasy becoming reality, swamped my head and my heart like never before.

Sarah would be loving this, I thought to myself. Forgetting, in the euphoria, that whatever she was loving was probably not going to be a concern of mine ever again.

The thought alone choked me. Gasping and my throat closed in on itself. I couldn't breathe. I crashed into a violent coughing fit and could feel my face burning red as I doubled over.

I might never see her again, I told myself.

"Are you alright mate?" the guy next to me asked. He was probably sixty, a longer sufferer than even most Coventry fans. In our greatest moment, he had found time to show concern for a fellow fan.

I nodded between coughing, bending over, and spitting on the floor.

"Here," he said, and offered me a can of Fosters. He gestured I should take a swig and that he wasn't offering me the whole can. I thanked him and took enough to wet my dry throat. The players were celebrating in front of us, but I wasn't able to join in.

Minutes later Bennett again goes down the right-wing, shadowed by both Micky Adams and John Stiles. He nutmegs Adams and is past Stiles before he even knows what's happened. His cross finds Houchen, whose first touch is superb, and sets up his shot nicely. He goes for the far post, but an outstretched leg clears it.

We were attacking at will now and it was Leeds players who were on the back foot. Their fans upped that aggressive roar and the City fans' response was as loud as thunder.

Now we had a game on our hands.

The stakes couldn't be higher, the tension was unbearable.

Something had to give.

There was going to be a winner.

And there was going to be a loser.

Seconds later and there was a scramble on the edge of the Leeds box. Mickey Gynn has worked his way across the eighteen-yard line and was fighting bravely against four Leeds defenders, all of which were twice his size. It seemed Gynn's heroics had been for nothing when David Rennie took a swing at the ball, intending his clearance to reach the back of the side-stand, but Rennie missed it completely.

And the ball rolled into the path of Roy of the Rovers, or Keith Houchen as he was also known, and this time, instead of shooting, he took it round the advancing Mervyn Day and slotted it home as a despairing Micky Adams slid across the goal line.

It was an explosion of joy and relief that raised the roof of the Kop and the purest form of the ecstasy descended onto each and every Coventry fan. Houchen, both arms out, received the admiration of the City faithful, and was mobbed by his teammates and we were in front for the first time.

We had twelve minutes to hold on and we'd be going to Wembley.

We lasted six.

Somehow, Andy Ritchie got the better of both Greggie Downs and Mickey Gynn and chipped in a cross from the bi-line. An unmarked Keith Edwards, the substitute who had been on the pitch all of two minutes, buried the ball into our net.

The other half of the stadium became a writhing mass of arms and bodies and the roar hit us like a tidal wave. Just seconds before we were nervously dreaming of the Twin Towers and now the history books would be re-written with the headline 'Six Minutes Away From Wembley'.

Although it felt like it, we weren't losing, but we were heading for extra-time.

It ended two-each at full-time and we had to wait for a nerve-shredding fifteen minutes or so for the break. The players formed two camps on the pitch and 50,00 fans took a seat and waited. John Sillett and George Curtis, the spirit and backbone of this team, breathed life into tired legs and fortified belief in beating hearts.

As I waited, with no action to distract me, the events of the day began to replay in my mind. The stupidity of the van-hire, the argument with Sarah's dad, seeing Sarah drive off with her boyfriend, and the real-life near-disaster on the motorway.

I considered trying to find Sarah's dad and making some amends. Amongst the twenty thousand on the Kop, it would be like trying to find a needle in a hundred haystacks after a hurricane, but at least I could say I tried. Obviously her dad would give his side of the story and I wasn't going to sugar-coat anything that I'd said, quite the opposite. And, besides, she had made her choice. That much was also obvious.

I thought about trying to find the lads, but even if I found them, I didn't have the heart to tell them they were right and I was wrong. All of which was true, but there's only so much truth a man can take in one day.

Instead, I sat on my piece of the terrace and stared at my feet.

This was not how I imagined things would be; being so close to the thing that I had dreamed of for all these years, and being alone. Was I paying a price for seeing my dream come true?

Finally, the ref gave the signal for the players to get back on their feet and the crowd-roar rose again.

I said a brief prayer to the football gods; You've let us come this far and in thirty minutes, our fate will have been decided. Please let us win. Even if we get relegated to Division Four in the future, I don't care. Just, please, let us win today. Thank you.

And they listened. And they answered.

Eight minutes into extra-time, at the far end of the ground, Benno was fouled just outside the box. Gynny floated a cross high to the far edge of the six-yard box for Cyril to head back across the goal. Houchen pounced with the outside of his boot and it struck Mervyn Day's chest only to land very neatly at the feet of one David Bennett who did not hesitate and poked it into the net.

In one-hundred-and-four years, this was the most important goal ever scored by Coventry City. For the fans, it was pandemonium, hysteria, all our emotions running riot. It was almost too much to comprehend. Our hearts weren't used to this violent roller-coaster that would hand us a dream then snatch it away. I thought, someone's probably having a heart-attack right now. There was some maniacal laughter all around me and even the eternal pessimists couldn't quite believe their eyes.

The history books were out again for another rewrite.

We got to the change of ends still in front.

The match kicked off for what I hoped would be the last time.

After ten long minutes, we were literally seconds away from our greatest result, but our tattered nerves could hardly bear it.

Sill the question had to be asked: Could it really be taken away from us again?

The answer was: Yes, it could.

And it so nearly was.

At the far end again, Keith Edwards latched onto a ball on the edge of the six-yard box with Oggy to beat, but the best keeper we ever had was quick of his feet and even quicker down to Edward's feet, arms outstretched, risking damage to his handsome-chiselled features. He turned the shot away for a corner the instant it left Edward's boot.

That had to be it. Surely. Even the tackiest Hollywood scriptwriter would say at that point, 'Enough with the drama'.

It took two minutes and an eternity, but finally, the referee put his whistle to his lips and blew full time.

We had done it.

It didn't feel real, but at the same time, it was the most real thing I had ever seen at a football match.

The players celebrated with the fans and mates hugged mates and people hugged strangers.

Dreams really do come true. We were going to Wembley.

All the scares along the way were something we could look back on and laugh about.

And all the disappointments over the years didn't seem to matter anymore because we were now on top of the world.

I applauded and screamed as long as my arms and lungs would let me and then I cried. I let the tears stream down my face. I didn't even have the strength to wipe them away, and I didn't want to. And I wasn't the only one, but for me, they were tears of both joy and sadness.

For gain and loss.

Dreams do come true.

But not all of them.

<< << > >>>

I was one of the last to leave the ground that day. Not because I wanted to prolong the celebrations, which had soon moved to outside the ground once the players had taken their party to the dressing room, but because I wanted to be alone.

I wasn't depressed, just exhausted. I was happy to watch the families and groups of mates having the time of their lives.

This was all about the city of Coventry. The day was ours and ours alone.

It was a long walk back from that cathedral of football, back to my Movies To You van. As I turned the key and the engine fired-up, I took in the site of Hillsborough Stadium, still bathed in floodlights, the battleground of our greatest triumph.

This will never ever happen again, I told myself.

And didn't I know it?

CHAPTER FIFTEEN

Monday 13th April 1987

"Something came up with my uni project," Sarah said. "An opportunity I couldn't miss. I'm sorry. I told my dad to explain everything."

We were in the round Wimpey and had eaten in silence.

Someone had once said, Never ask a question that you don't already know the answer to. So I'd asked her why she didn't show up for the Leeds game.

She wouldn't tell me on the phone. She said she wanted to see me. I was supposed to be flattered by that request.

"And how did it go?"

She seemed surprised at the question, but told me it went well. "I pitched my idea to a company who makes plastic car parts and they liked it, so, yes, it went well."

I knew she was lying.

"That's great," I said.

"It was great," she said. "They're going to donate to the project and sign up to take part once things get up and running."

"Yeah, OK," I said, "I don't really need the details."

"Look Steve, I told my dad to explain it to you and to say how sorry I was. I thought at least you guys could go to the game together. You didn't need me there, anyway."

"Well, it didn't work out that way," I said, "I don't think I'll be playing happy families with your dad any time soon."

"What happened?"

"Or your brother," I added, ignoring her question.

"I understand you're pissed off at me," she said. "I just wanted you to know how important this Uni work is to me and that it was a last-minute thing and I couldn't miss it."

"You couldn't phone the Taj to let me know?"

"I didn't have their number."

"It's in the phone-book," I said. I hated being this harsh to her, although I had every right to be, considering she was still lying to me and had been all along. She was just getting better at it.

"I'm sorry, I didn't think." She had given up explaining now. "I had that one thing on my mind. And I'm sorry. I apologise."

I nodded and got up to leave. "Yeah, thanks," I said. "I'm off to the match."

She looked up and nodded.

"Will you get home alright?" I asked.

She nodded again.

Despite myself, I still felt sorry for her. I couldn't just walk away and leave things like this.

"I'll call you," I said.

"Please do," she said. "Please."

"And Sarah," I said, "speak to your dad again, ask him to be honest with you about what happened."

"What? Tell me!"

"Just ask him to tell you the truth."

CHAPTER SIXTEEN

Wednesday 22nd April 1987

I rang Sarah on Wednesday after doing the video round on my own again.

She asked how I was and we both said sorry.

That Monday we played QPR at home and it was the best home game of the season.

We were going to Wembley, in a good position in the league, and playing with a flair and freedom that I'd never seen before.

We scored four goals that day and could have easily scored six or seven. It was one of those perfect games when everything went right.

But I was miserable.

I reminded Sarah that I was going to get our Cup Final tickets next Monday.

"I don't need to be there, do I?" she said.

"No, I've got your ticket stubs, so I can get both of ours, no problem."

"Good, because I have to do a presentation at the Uni on Monday and it will go into the evening."

"No problem," I said, "I'll probably be queuing all day anyway, so I'll catch up with you later."

"I'm going to need to lock myself away and do a lot of work for this thing, though. I won't see you until afterwards, is that OK?"

I nodded, "I'll cope, somehow."

"This is the last bit of uni for the year and I've got a lot to do, but I'll be free after that. We can spend more time together."

"You're still coming to the Final then?"

"Yes," she said, "of course." Then she added, "If you want me to."

"Why wouldn't I?"

We were both silent for a moment.

"Sorry," I said. "That sounded wrong. I gotta go."

I put the phone down.

CHAPTER SEVENTEEN

Saturday 25th April 1987

"Your mum says there's a wedding in a few weeks," Molly said.

"Yeah. You heard about that, did you?"

"She mentioned it."

"And what did she say?"

Molly shook her head and waved a heavily lacquered finger at me. "You don't get to ask the questions," she said.

"Well," I sighed, "Ask me no questions and I'll tell you no lies."

"Your mum's not going to like it, Steve," she told me. "You do know that, don't you?"

I nodded.

The market was busy, and Shirley was only just coping with the customers. Molly was too polite to ask me to leave, but I knew better than to hang around and get in the way.

"Do you need any more flags and stuff?" I asked.

She nodded, "If you can get 'em, I can sell 'em."

"Cool, if I can I'll have them for you on Monday."

I got up to leave.

"I'd best get out of your way," I told her.

She got up and slipped her hand into her jeans pocket and took out a roll of notes.

"This is yours," she said. "For the Levi's."

I took it.

"I've still got some left if you're interested."

"No thanks," she said. Then added, "No harm done, but I'd get rid of whatever you've got left if I were you."

"Why? What you heard?"

"Nothing really, just whispers," she said, "but there's no smoke without fire. Better safe than sorry."

I didn't need to hear any more. "A nod's as good as a wink to a blind bat," I smiled.

She lifted the counter and I stepped down from the stall.

When I turned to her, she was no longer smiling.

"Anyway," she said, "Good luck."

I gave her a thumbs up, put my palms together and bowed gratefully.

CHAPTER EIGHTEEN

Sunday 26th April

The tea that Bal's mum made was always strong, thick enough to stand the spoon in, and the little cakes that she baked were a gorgeous blend of sweet and savoury that melted in the mouth. In the fifteen years that I'd known her, she'd always worn traditional Indian dress, elegant clothing that she had handmade.She rarely spoke but would always ask me how I was and whether I wanted any more tea, cakes, and no doubt a three-course-meal, if I asked for it.

Me, Bal and Barrath were at the dining-room table and once she had decided that I had eaten enough cakes, she left us to our discussion.

I took a sip of tea. It was hot. As I blew the steam away, I glanced at Barrath.

He looked nervous, but not quite as shy as he normally was.

I wanted to give him some good news, and some cash from the sale of the computer games, but neither of those two things were going to happen. Not today anyway.

Bal had The Sun spread out on the table and, starting at the back, he was working his way through every football article.

I couldn't keep Barrath waiting any longer. I put my cup down and sat up in the chair.

"So mate," I said, "I'm sorry to say, things didn't work out as we planned."

He frowned. "What do you mean?"

"Well, I took the games to the market and done the deal to sell a few," I said, "and they sold a few."

"So? That's good, isn't it?"

"Yes and no mate," I said, "Yes and no."

"I don't understand," he said, pushing himself away from the table so his chair swung back on its back legs.

"The guy who runs the store took them home to test them out," I explained, "and he told me he found what he called 'Bugs' in them."

"Bugs?" Barrath said. He let his chair drop back to earth on its four legs and leant across the table, his eyes fixed on mine. "What kind of bugs?"

"What are bugs?" Bal asked, without looking up from his newspaper.

"I can't give the technical terms, but he said that in the King Arthur game, after the Lady of the Lake gave him Excalibur, he has to fight off twenty Aston Villa fans in a pub called The Miners Arms. So it seems we got the games mixed up."

"Oh, shit!" Barrath gasped. "Are you for real?" He looked truly panicked by this news.

I nodded.

"There's similar 'bugs' in some of the other games, but I forget the exact details."

"I'm so sorry, Steven," Barrath whispered, "I'm so stupid."

"I don't think you're stupid," I said, "quite the opposite."

Barrath's hands had gone to his scalp and grabbed a fistful of hair. I let out a low moan that turned into words that I guessed were him swearing in Indian, but I had no idea what he was saying. Each syllable came out through gritted teeth and seemed to consist of pure shame.

"Barrath, look at me."

Shame had now turned to anger.

I told him, "So I agreed to bring back the stock he has left and that we would correct these bug things."

He stared at me without answering.

"Can you fix these bugs?" I asked him. To me, the word bugs still sounded wrong coming out of my mouth. All I could picture were actual bugs like beetles and earwigs. This was Barrath's language, not mine.

"Yes. I can fix them, but they shouldn't have been there in the first place. We should have done thorough beta testing."

"That doesn't matter. All that matters is that you can fix the bugs?"

"Yes," he nodded, "we can fix them and rewrite the disks. I'll work through the night-"

"No, no, you don't need to do that," I laughed, "take as long as you need and don't beat yourself up about this."

"Too late for that," Bal commented.

"Shut up, you!" Barrath told him.

"Now listen," I told him.

"I've let you down, haven't I?"

"No," I said, "not at all, mate. The guy absolutely loved the games. He wants more, just without the bugs. To be honest, I didn't think any of this was going to work and I don't know how, but I'm so glad that you did, because this feels like something big. Really big. This bug-thing is a minor setback. If we can get over this, I think we could sell more of these disks, a lot more."

Barrath looked stunned.

"If you're up for it?" I asked.

Bal looked up from the paper and looked at his brother.

"Yeah, I'm up for it," Barrath said, "I'm totally up for it."

As I left Bal's house, he offered me a lift to my mum's.

I declined. "Thanks, but the longer I delay this conversation, the better."

"You're telling her today?" Bal asked.

I nodded and he winced.

"Good luck mate," he said.

"I'm gonna need it."

An hour later, I was in mum's kitchen. The radio was on. She'd been doing her housework when I arrived. Derek was on his way to Bournemouth, it being Sunday night.

She didn't offer me a coffee, so I assumed she knew what was coming. She'd probably known what was coming all along, but mothers somehow find a glimmer of hope where there's not even a chink of light.

"So, you've made your mind up then?" she said.

Her Sunday jumper had been discarded onto the kitchen table and she wore a grey T-shirt that reflected her mood.

I nodded. "First, I wanna say that the last thing I would ever want to do is hurt you, mum," I said, "and if there was any other way to sort this out, then I'd do anything-"

"There is another way," she said, "there's always been another way, it's very simple-"

"Mum!" I said, "I just can't."

She folded her arms, lent back against the kitchen side and dropped her chin down to her chest.

We were both silent for a at least half a minute. I had nothing else to add. Mum had plenty and was obviously considering her words.

She lifted her head and asked me, "Can I ask you something?"

I nodded.

"Do you know how much this hurts me?"

"Yes."

"I mean, do you really know? Do you understand what it means to me?" Her eyes had found mine and wouldn't let go. "This isn't about you not being with me on a particular day when I really need you to be. This isn't about the humiliation that I will have to face. This is about you knowing how much you are hurting me, and doing it anyway."

I had no answer. I had reasons, but they weren't good enough for her and we both knew it.

I'd never seen my mum cry, not ever. I'd seen her receive devastating news, Id seen her at family funerals, and I'd seen her bear the greatest sadness, but she never cried. 'Only when I'm alone,' she had once said. But this was the closest that I'd seen.

"So let me ask you again, because I want us to be absolutely crystal clear on this," she said, her voice cracking with dryness. "Do you know how much this hurts me?"

"Mum, please-" I started to say.

"It's an easy question, Steven!" she shouted. "Do you? Or don't you?"

I couldn't answer. I said nothing.

Mum shook her head and unfolded her arms. Her anger was gone. She'd moved on.

"OK," she said. "I have things to do so-"

"It wasn't easy."

"You can cut the bullshit, Steven," she said. "Why can't you be honest? It was the easiest decision you ever had to make. It took a split-second for you to make up your mind."

"You don't understand," I said.

"You're right, I don't understand, because, after all I've done for you, this is the one time I ask you to do something for me, but you can't be bothered. If I was in your place, I wouldn't do that. So, no, I don't understand. But you go ahead. You've made your decision. I don't like it and I definitely do not respect it, or you come to that, but you're an adult. I can't force you to do things any more. I can only explain what the right thing to do is and ask you to do it."

I looked at the floor.

Her voice was quieter now, almost soothing. "I tried to raise you to know the difference between choosing what's right and what's best. Clearly I failed."

I had to have one go at explaining, but wasn't sure where to start, so I tried to start at the beginning.

I looked up. She was calm now, resigned to her fate, picking up the pieces and moving forward.

"Do you remember the first game I went to?"

She exhaled and her lips raised.

"You made me wear that red scarf so I didn't catch a cold."

She turned away, grabbed a tea-towel and started drying the dishes.

"It was the scarf or stay at home," I said. "And I chose the scarf and went to the game."

She had her back to me and was organising the washing up. Plates were clattered together and cupboard doors flung open.

"And I wanted to go, because it was what dad did," I said, "going to the football was-"

Mum exploded with rage. The plate in her hand slammed into the cupboard, shattering into fragments.

"Don't you dare! Do not blame your father for your selfish behaviour!"

She stormed across the room. Her face was inches from mine. There were tears on her cheeks and what was left of the plate in her hand.

"Your father wouldn't even dream of putting football before family. He would never put anything before his wife and child, and he would be disgusted by you! He would be truly repulsed by what you're doing."

"No, mum," I said. I could feel my own tears in my eyes. "No!"

"What's up Steve?" she asked. "I thought you were adult enough to stand by your decisions now? I don't need to protect you from the truth anymore, do I? You can take it, right? You're a man now, aren't you?"

"Mum, stop!"

She grabbed my wrist with her free hand and leaned closer to me. With each word, I felt her breath and spit on my face.

"And I'll tell you something else, shall I?" she hissed. "He wouldn't be that happy with what you're doing with his money."

I couldn't believe what she was saying. I went into shock.

"Don't you think I know you're selling stolen goods and dodgy computer games on the market? And your stupid Video Delivery Service, what a joke. That's not a business, Steven, that's not working for a living. It's pathetic. And you probably think you're a business genius, but you're not, are you? We just let you pretend you're a genius whilst we waited for you to grow-up!"

I could only let the tears flow and stare at this person as she tore me apart.

She let go of my hand.

"And now we don't need to wait anymore, do we?" she said.

She reached to the table and handed me a tissue.

"My little boy, all grown-up."

She threw the broken plate in the sink and left the room.

I was shell-shocked. I couldn't control my trembling. My dried tears have gummed up my eyes and my nose was dripping snot like a tap.

After a few minutes, mum came back in the kitchen and turned the radio up.

She hummed along to Reet Petite as she put on her marigolds and cleaned up the broken crockery from the sink.

That done, she finished the drying up and folded the tea-towel.

The song finished and the DJ spoke to us, "Before we go to Mercia Sound news, I just want to let you know that we're getting reports of fans already queuing down at Highfield Road for F.A. Cup Final tickets. It's estimated that over a thousand people are already there and will be staying overnight before the ticket office opens in the morning-"

233

Mum turned the radio off.

"You'd better get down there," she said. "You don't want to miss out."

Although I was broken, she was her normal self now. Or at least her new self. She was definitely changed.

"I'd give you a lift, but Derek's got the car."

I got to my feet and wiped my nose again.

"Bye Steve," she smiled.

"Bye mum."

$<<<<$ $>>>>$

I got the bus from Bedworth to Pool Meadow and walked up Cox Street to the bedsit.

I knew that by rights I should try to let Andy and Chris and Bal know the queues were forming and they needed to get down there, but I was still in a state and didn't want them to see how messed up I was. There was no way I could hide it from them and it was also fair to say that I wasn't going to share their total enthusiasm for the FA Cup Final ticket purchase experience.

I had known that the conversation with mum was going to be difficult for both of us and very emotional, but I was not prepared for how ferociously she would turn on me. I'd seen her like that maybe two or three times before, but always in my defence. I'd never been the one staring down the barrel before.

I'd expected her to guilt-trip me into changing my mind, and that wasn't going to happen. And I didn't disagree with what she'd said, but the most frightening part of it all was how calm she was after. I was devastated and on the verge of my tears when I thought about mum, but I knew she's be watching TV with a glass of wine and planning tomorrow's workday and what's for tea.

< < < <   > > > >

I got to a floodlit Highfield Road at about ten o'clock and there were people everywhere.

Corner shops were open and people were queuing down the street. Kids were playing Continental in the club car park and the stewards on the gates were trying to stop people from wandering anywhere they shouldn't.

The queue itself started at the ticket office, went into the ground, ran all the way down the Sky Blue terrace and then spread onto the Kop.

I took up a spot at the top of the terrace and settled down to watch and wait.

At some point, the floodlights were turned down just dim enough to light the stadium.

There were probably two thousand people there by that time, and some people had come more prepared than others. Many had sleeping bags, blankets, even a gas stove, others were shivering in the T-shirts and Harrington jackets they'd been wearing when they heard the news. I had my ski-jacket on, chosen more because it covered my head with its hood, but I was already glad of its warmth.

Spirits started off high. This was a once-in-a-lifetime event. Even if by some miracle we got to another Cup Final, this would always be the first, and that made it a rite of passage another unique occasion to be savoured.

As I looked around, I saw card games, picnics and couples cuddling. A game of head-tennis developed into a five-a-side kick-about on the terrace which, due to the inevitable Sunday-League level of control, resulted in the ball flying over the steel fence and onto the pitch. There was a collective sigh from both sides, then a small party ventured down to retrieve it and found that the gate was unlocked. The one lad dashed onto the pitch and grabbed the ball, to the collective cheers of the crowd, and drop-kicked it back on to the terrace.

In less than two minutes, the ball was back on the pitch and this time it took three lads to retrieve it, but before they could do so, they could not resist taking a penalty, and missed.

The crowd jeered and another thirty or so spilled onto the pitch to show them how it's done.

Within minutes, the box was filled with about a hundred fans all trying to get on the end of a cross from the left wing.

Not surprisingly, there were very few goals for those of us remaining on the terrace to cheer and the fun ended when the floodlights came on in full glare and the groundsman ran over from the tunnel shouting 'Gerrof the pitch'.

Giggling like schoolboys, the players all ran to the gate and retreated to the terrace.

I spotted Chris and Andy. They were the last to leave, Andy scoring with a header, then throwing the ball back to Chris, who missed from eight yards out.

I wanted to join them, or part of me did, but a bigger part of me wanted to be alone.

Sarah was the person I really wanted to be with. She was the only one who would understand what I was going through with mum, but there was no way I was asking her to spend the night on a football terrace queuing for tickets. Besides, I had her stubs so I could her ticket with mine and we could go to Wembley together.

I wondered if she was with Greg right now. I wondered why she was treating me like a mug and being so nice about it.

I huddled up. It was getting cold, the laughter had stopped. Blankets, food and a warm drink were now much sort-after commodities. Word got round that the corner shops had all closed for the night. People were sleeping. Other people were walking into sleeping people. Tempers were flaring. Singing and shouting was met with orders to shut up, arguments were starting and a few altercations broke out. Everyone was tired, cold and knackered.

This was going to get all 'Lord of the flies', I thought to myself. There was another nine hours of it yet.

CHAPTER NINETEEN

Monday 27th April 1987

I got to The Lanch at gone three on Monday afternoon. I'd been awake for over thirty-hours by that time. I sneaked in and find a comfy place to crash whilst I waited for Sarah.

There was hardly anyone about and those that passed me by were hurrying toward a bank of double-doors marked 'Presentation Hall'.

I decided to see if I could find her inside.

There were banks of chairs in the hall and on a stage with side curtains some guy was talking into a microphone about 'the strength and determination that this years recipient has demonstrated not only in her university course work, but in local business and the community.'

The audience were all ears and no one paid much attention to me as I slipped into a chair.

"So ladies and gentlemen, please put your hands together for the Founder of Helping Hands Foundation, Miss Sarah Morales."

I think the word is 'surreal'. I was so exhausted I wasn't sure if I was hallucinating, but there she was. I could see her plain as day, on the stage, thanking the companies that had already pledged support for her project to the tune of twenty-thousand pounds.

"I can't thank those companies enough for having faith in me," Sarah said. "And I will do all I can to repay their trust in me."

She looked different. Her hair was up. I'd never seen it done like that before. There was no track suit top, no jeans or white high-top trainers. She wore a dark blue business-suit, tight pencil skirt, black stockings and heels. She looked every inch the sharp business executive.

Was this the same girl who was going to get excited that I'd got her a Cup Final ticket?

And why hadn't she told me about getting this award? It looked to me like a big deal. I wondered where the twenty-grand has came from. She was talking in front of about three hundred people, and I could hear a pin drop.

I could grasp parts of what she was saying, but my concentration was dipping in and out as I tried to answer the stream of questions I kept asking myself.

She was reading from some small cards.

"...and we believe it is possible that, given a helping hand, that we can employ the unemployed. That a company does not have to exist for the sole purpose of generating profit. A company can exist 'Not For Profit', to benefit the community, to benefit the people that matter within that community, and it can still be more efficient, more resourceful and more competitive than the companies that exist to feed fat-cats."

Round of applause. I joined in.

"Thank you," she said, "Thank you all so much."

She stepped away from the microphone and people got to their feet as they continued their round of applause.

I climbed on my chair and wolf-whistled, cheered like we'd won the Cup already.

I shouted her name.

And she saw me.

And then I remembered.

Helping Hands.

The brochure.

It was hers.

I could hear myself saying to her, 'Well, it's not the best idea in the world, is it? How would it ever work?'

And 'It's a nice idea for a university student to dream up, but the real world doesn't work like that.'

And 'If students want to understand what the under-privileged need, they should ask them what they want, not play games in a university class-room.'

And I think at that same moment she could hear those words too.

I got down from the chair before I fell down.

I found her having photographs taken with a stream of well-wishers, businessmen, and university people.

I waited for her to accept their congratulations and praise.

It took a long time.

She ushered me into a small dressing-room with a smile and a promise of being five minutes max.

"You look great," I said, but she'd gone.

She was seven minutes.

In that time, I had gone from bursting with pride to burning with shame. I could not understand why she hadn't told me. It would have been embarrassing for me, not her. I had been critical. She could have at least rubbed my nose in it, but she said nothing.

And I thought she was a terrible liar, which was something else I'd been proven totally wrong about.

Maybe if she'd kept that promise of five minutes, it would've been different, who knows. It was probably in the last two minutes that the jealousy crept in. But coming off of yesterday's arse-kicking by my mum, and still not having slept since, it was a bitter pill to find out that my quiet but cute student girlfriend had achieved more in the last few months than I probably would in years.

And the jealous voice whispered in my head, "Yes, but it's not a level playing field, is it? So it's not really a fair fight.

No, I insisted of myself, her achievement was incredible, she deserves this and it shouldn't even be a fight, so fair or not doesn't come into it.

"Well, yes, all of that is true, no denying it," the jealous voice said. "I'm just saying she had the advantage."

No, no, no. Don't say it.

But the jealous voice said it anyway and I couldn't deny that the jealousy was part of me. "She has privilege. So you had no chance. That's why she won't rub your nose in it; she doesn't want to lower herself to your level."

And that was when she'd came back into the room.

"I wasn't expecting you this early," she said.

There'd been no hug, not even a smile.

"What was that?" I asked, nodding over her shoulder at what was outside the door. I had intended it as a compliment, but it hadn't come out sounding like one.

She looked away.

"So are you like Student of the Year or something?" I smiled, "That's great Sarah. You must be very-" It still didn't sound right, "-proud of yourself."

She looked back at me, then said, "I am."

And I looked away.

I was too tired to say the right thing, except, "Sorry, I shouldn't have come."

"Look, Steve," she'd said, "it's great that you're here. It's great to see you, but I'm going to be here for a while, so can we meet later?"

"Yeah sure," I said. "I've been up all night queuing for our tickets, so I should probably get my head down. I'll be at the bedsit."

"You got the tickets then?" she asked.

"Yes," I said.

She smiled and nodded, took three steps to the side of the room, her heels clicking on the hard floor, her arms folded, head down.

Still no hug, and I wasn't going to beg.

I made my way to the door. "You do know that I was joking, right?" I said, "All that stuff about your student project."

She was wearing a lot of make-up. She looked nice, but very different, less fun.

"Of course," she forced a smiled.

I forced a smile of my own and turned to the door.

And that was when Greg walked in.

"Sarah, your presence is requested-"

He was exactly how I remember him that day I first met her. A silky smooth wedge and a flash suit. Smarmy was the first word that came to mind, and there were plenty more that followed.

We stared at each other for a while. He knew who I was and I knew who he was.

"You're in my way," I told him, taking a step to the door.

"Steve, wait!" Sarah said.

I looked back. She may have had a tear forming. It was hard to tell.

"Don't cry," I said to her, "It'll ruin your makeup."

She closed her eyes and pushed her lips together as she turned away.

"You're still in my way," I told Greg.

He looked at Sarah, who must've made a signal behind my back, and he stepped aside.

I didn't bother with any emotional farewells.

I just left.

CHAPTER TWENTY

Saturday 2nd May 1987

"Fiver a frame?" my new scouse mate asked. "Make it ind'restin'"

I nodded, "Sure mate."

It was one o'clock and I'd found Andy and Chris in the Mercer's Arms. They hadn't told me they were going for a pre-match pint and they didn't look too pleased to see me, but, as I told them, they'd get over it.

It was Cov fans only in the lounge at The Mercers, but back room was always packed with home and away fans on match days and it had six pool tables. I was no Steve Davis, but I'd seen The Color Of Money and pool looked like an easy game to me, even after three pints.

"Do you want me to break?" I asked, immediately handing him a huge advantage, but my tactics were more about psychological intimidation than skill with the cue.

He nodded, "Go for it."

He racked the balls up as I spotted the white ball and practiced my cuing action.

"Me name's John," he said, as I was about to break.

"Steve," I said, not looking up.

I cracked the cue ball into the pack and it exploded in all directions, but none of them found a pocket.

I remained philosophical about it, certain that I'd do better on my return to the table. First, I needed to retrieve my beer, as that would loosen me up.

As I sipped my drink, I heard a ball hit the back of the pocket and before I'd finished, another followed it. I turned to look in time to see the third slowly topple over the edge of the middle. Then he potted another. He hadn't moved from the spot yet. He was picking off stripe balls like a sniper in a clock tower.

When he missed his fourth shot, he had covered the corner pocket and despite all the spots being still on the table, I didn't have a clean shot at any of them.

Safety it is then, I thought, and attempted to roll the white up to a red spot on the side cushion creating a nice snooker, but alas, it was fractionally over-hit and there was daylight between my red ball and the cushion, enough for John to thread the cue ball through and pot the ball he'd just seconds ago placed on the cusp of the pocket.

"Shot!" I said. But it wasn't that good.

John's mates were laughing.

My mates had Dunkirked and were nowhere to be seen.

John cleaned up and as the black ambled in to the pocket, he asked, "Again?"

"Your break," I nodded, and waved my empty pint glass to signal I was going to get another.

Some time later, when Andy reappeared, I had a fresh pint and was halfway through another frame.

"What you doing?" he asked me.

"What's it look like?"

"Game's starting," he said, "Come on."

"I'll just finish my beer and game of pool, if that's alright with you," I told him.

"Game's over," Andy said.

I didn't even need to look around to know that John had just sunk the black again and was waiting to receive the victor's spoils. I'd lost count of the number of fivers I'd handed over, six or seven, I guess.

"Drink up," Andy ordered, his voice getting condescending.

I finished the pint, stuck the empty on the bar, and fished out another fiver for John.

"Good game mate," I said, "thanks."

"Thank you!" he said.

There was no need to rub it in.

"Goin' to Wembley, are ya?" he said.

"Yeah," I said, "Are you?"

He placed his pool cue on the table and took a step toward me. "Do you even know where Wembley is?"

Andy grabbed my arm and marched me away. I didn't put up much of a struggle and John was laughing as he shouted, "See ya next season, yeah Steve? We can have a rematch? Bring your money, yeah?"

Coventry won one-nil. It was a shame I didn't get to see John again after the match. Nick Pickering scored, making sure that Gary Gillespie's return to Highfield Road wasn't a pleasant one. It wasn't a particularly pleasant return for me, either. I wasn't used to drinking in the afternoon.

CHAPTER TWENTY-ONE

Sunday 3rd May 1987

I rang her.

"We can't leave it like this," I told her.

"OK, how do you want to leave it?"

"Sarah, I don't want to leave it at all."

"Oh, so you've had a change of heart?"

That hurt. "No."

I left her some silence to fill with words if she wanted to.

I counted to ten, almost, then she said, "Where do you want to meet?"

< < < <   > > > >

We met in the park.

I knew that I'd let her down somehow, but also that she hadn't trusted me enough, or, worse, she didn't want me to know.

"Why didn't you tell me about your project?" I asked her.

"It was something I had to," she said.

"I could've helped you," I said, then corrected myself, "supported you."

"It was something I had to do alone."

"You thought I'd-"

"You already said so, Steve," she told me. "'Best leave Social justice to the downtrodden', wasn't that your advice?"

"I didn't mean-"

"What did you mean?"

She looked at me as her eyes welled up with tears.

"I needed someone who believed in me," she said, "and you weren't ready for that. I know that's not your fault, because it was something I'd started before we met. And I wanted to finish it."

"You make me sound like I would have stopped you-"

"You would," she said, "like I say, that's not your fault, but I didn't want any excuses."

She wasn't even trying to stop the tears now. They rolled down her cheeks, each burning like acid.

She sobbed and sniffed, shook her head.

"It's what I do," she said. "If I'd told you, it would happen again."

"Sarah, I don't understand," I pleaded. "What would happen?"

She shook her head in a rage. "Don't you know? Haven't you figured me out yet?" she shouted, "I figured you out in five minutes Steve, and you still know nothing about me after five months!"

"Not true," I said.

"So what is it then? What is it I always do in the end?"

"Why don't you tell me-"

"I quit," she said and instantly seemed relieved just saying the words. "I never 'finish' anything. I quit because I don't have the confidence to see things through. I don't have the guts-"

"How can you 'not' have confidence?" I said, "Look at you! How can you 'not' believe in yourself? Look at all the things you've done."

"I haven't 'done' anything," she yelled. "I've been given everything. I never achieved one thing in my life. And I just wanted this one thing to be mine, one thing that I did, by myself, without him taking over and taking it away from me! And then I'd say to him, 'See! Look what I did! And I did it on my own!'"

"Who? Greg?"

"What! No! My dad! He takes over everything I do. Pulling strings and favours-" Then she froze and looked up at me. "Did you say 'Greg'?"

"Yeah, Greg," I said.

"What about him?"

I shook my head in disbelief.

"It's Greg's company, Steve," she said.

"Yeah, yeah, it's Greg's company," I nodded, dripping in sarcasm.

"What's that supposed to mean?"

"That's supposed to mean, how come you never told me you're still seeing him?"

"I'm not!"

"Stop lying, Sarah, let's just be honest with each other."

"I am being honest!"

"I saw you Sarah," I said. "The day of the semi-final, when you said you had that last-minute-thing to do with the University project, I saw you. Your dad told me you were with Greg and I went to your house and I saw you!"

"No, Steve, my dad didn't even know-"

"Stop lying! Please, Sarah, just stop. Jordan heard you on the phone arranging to meet Greg."

"I am not lying. The meeting was for my Helping Hands project. Greg was involved because it was his company and I could only do it that Sunday when dad was out. He was going to be at the football all day, it was the only time-"

"So you were seeing him and me at the same time? How's that for social justice in action? It's OK to cheat as long as it's you that's doing it. Well I'm not gonna be your mug any more, and don't pretend you're heartbroken. You've had your fun."

"You!" she said. "How can you-"

She raised an accusing finger, intended for me, then dropped it to her side.

She raised her head, turned and walked away.

CHAPTER TWENTY-TWO

Monday 4th May 1987

I was running from Filbert Street amid fights breaking out all over the place.

Due to the Cup Run, City had a backlog of fixtures to get through and that meant two mid-week games, Leicester away on the Monday night and Man Utd at home on Wednesday.

The Leicester game was too close to home to miss. Thousands of Coventry fans had made the journey and I travelled up the M69 with Chris, Andy, Bal and Barrath, who joined us for his first away game.

Bal had offered to drive, assuring us that the Viva was now a crushed cube in a scrap yard by the Foleshill gasworks, and that we'd be taking the Mk3 Escort.

Bal picked me up first.

Barrath looked nervous as I ruffled his hair. "You ready for this?"

"I'm ready," he said.

When we picked Chris up, he looked at me and got straight to the point. "You look like shit mate, did you break up with your bird?"

I didn't even try to evade the question. I didn't have the strength and I thought a straight guilty plea may avoid further questions. "Yeah," I told him, "something like that."

"Oh well," Chris consoled me, "best thing to do is to get back on the horse. Its Grab-A-Granny night at Fatty's this Thursday."

"Good to know," I said. "Thanks for the advice."

The lads tried to rekindle the old 'team spirit', but none of us were really feeling it. We were like a failed marriage, staying together for the kids. We laughed our way through, but none of us were under any illusions that things would go back to how they were.

< < < <   > > > >

Getting into Filbert Street had been worse than the Quarter Finals at Hillsborough. They shoved us into a pen behind the goal and it soon became jam-packed. The Leicester fans were on the other side of the terrace, and separated from us by two empty pens. Nobody could move and the squeeze was getting serious. There were long moments when the bodies around me were so packed that I felt a panic rising in my throat. My woolly-hat had fallen down over my left eye and I didn't have enough elbow room to raise my arms to push it back up. The noise was deafening. City songs mixed with cries of rage and I wondered if I lost control of whether anyone would hear my screams. I was only just holding onto my mind when someone reached over and lifted my hat. I didn't see who it was, but I thanked him.

I used to think this was fun, I thought. But then it was never like this. Now that Coventry had a big following, these things were becoming normal.

Once there was a break in the squeeze, I pushed my way to the side fence and climbed it to look at what was happening. Our pen was full beyond any sane capacity. There was literally no room left for more people, yet the stewards, aided by the police, were still pushing people in through the gate.

Barrath had followed me and was being pressed against the fence by the sheer weight of numbers. He looked terrified and close to panic.

"Get up here," I told him. "Climb up!"

I helped him climb up where at least he could breathe.

Then, not far from us, people were pointing. It took me a while to figure it out, but then I realised they were pointing at a gate to the empty pen beside us.

"Open the gate, for God's sake!" someone shouted.

More screamed the same thing.

I climbed the fence higher and looked around for a steward or policeman. The only ones I saw were shouting at me to get down. I gestured for them to come and get me if they wanted to, then pointed at the gate. Two policemen entered the pen and drew their truncheons as more of us climbed the fence and pointed at the gate.

As they approached, looking very much like they were about to enjoy shooting fish in a barrel, their expressions changed when they saw the wall of faces pressed against the fence. The steward pulled out a set of keys.

The gate was opened and hundreds of City fans poured through into the wide open space beside us.

As me and Barrath climbed down from the fence, I noticed that most of the Leicester fans had been enjoying our little spectacle and openly laughed and jeered at us. I couldn't blame them. We'd have done the same if the roles had been reversed, but I wondered what that said about all of us.

What if someone died at a football match? Would we still laugh and jeer as long as it wasn't us? Even as we looked at the body on the ground?

I didn't know the answer to that question. And I didn't want to know.

Apart from escaping with our lives, the game was memorable for the Mexican Waves created by the City fans. We now stretched around a full quarter of the ground and it was a spectacular distraction.

The game ended one-all. We were undefeated in five games and the team were looking good.

And so we waited to be released, the usual drill, and we filed out after the allotted time.

Everyone was jumpy. There was something in the air, and Filbert Street had always been a horrible place to get out of. Once you were away from the ground, the police weren't concerned for your welfare. And we were parked in a side street about ten minutes' walk away.

We made our way through the terraced streets spread out by about ten or twenty yards. I was with Barrath, Andy and Bal was ahead of us, Chris behind. The street-corners were blind, no way of knowing who or what was there. The trick was to keep walking as if you knew where you were going. Like a local.

"Alright, lads?"

A bloke had stepped out of one of the many narrow alleys and spoke in a low, inquisitive voice. He was stocky and ugly and wore a dark blue Fred Perry, no jacket, tight faded jeans, steel toe capped Docs. I guessed he wasn't nipping out to buy bread and milk.

"Alright," I said and kept walking, hoping that he would step aside.

Barrath hesitated and I reached out and took the elbow of his jacket to urge him on.

The bloke took that as the sign that he needed and spread his stanch to fill the whole pavement. "Where you heading, lads?"

I glanced over his shoulder to give him an indication of our intentions without speaking. Andy and Bal had carried on oblivious. By the time they'd look back, it would probably be too late.

"Going home," I said.

I stopped and stood just out of arms-reach. We were boxed in by a parked car, nowhere to go. Barrath, unable to stand still shuffled from one foot to the other, like he was treading water.

It was then that I saw Chris has crossed to the other side of the road. Like everyone else, he kept his head down and minded his own business.

"What's up, mate?" I said, hoping my accent wasn't too strong, but knowing that it probably was.

The bloke shrugged. "I just wanted to introduce myself," he said.

He raised his shoulders in what might have been intended to be a shrug, but was more like the shrug that Mike Tyson did when he came out of his corner to batter the shit out of the poor bastard in the other corner.

And that was when Chris walked up behind and gave him a sharp tap on the back of the head. That was our cue. His lights went out and he went down like a discarded puppet. I grabbed Barrath's arm and dragged him forward. We hurdled the fallen body and ran.

I was trying to make sense of what had just happened and all I could come with was the Chris had somehow developed a Vulcan death grip.

Then I saw what was he was stuffing into his pocket and it all made sense; the cosh. The thug had been hit in the head with a steel ball encased in hard rubber. No wonder he went down like a sack of shit.

"Don't run!" Chris hissed at us. "Walk!"

I walked. Fast.

I glanced behind, but there was no one there.

"Don't worry," Chris said, "he ain't coming after us for a while."

"Where are we?" Andy asked.

"No idea," Bal said.

"We go left at the end of this street," Chris said, "circle back and it's the second street on the right."

"Good," I said, then added, "Are you sure?"

"Not really," he said.

"Good enough."

CHAPTER TWENTY-THREE

Wednesday 6th May 1987

Manchester United at home was our third game in five days. The result wasn't much of a concern. We were safely mid-table and nothing to play for, but any injuries now would seriously weaken us come Cup Final day. Somebody should've told the players, especially Brian Kilcline and Lloyd McGrath, though, because they played like it was the Cup Final. They only had one way of playing and that was to commit one hundred per cent.

United had been useless all season, even by their own standards. They had lost four-nil to Tottenham on Monday night, (a reminder for us about how we could face a similar scoreline in ten days' time). Clive Allen had scored his forty-eighth goal of the season, more than any player in my lifetime. Many predicted that we would do much worse. 'Enjoy the build-up,' they said, 'cos once it kicks off, we'll have nothing to cheer'. Lesson One.

Fifteen minutes into the game and after an epic goal-mouth scramble, somehow we couldn't put the ball in the net. After twenty-four minutes, United managed to get a cross into the box and Norman Whiteside scored with a soft header. Strangely, knowing the result didn't matter, didn't make it hurt any less.

In the second half, Bryan Robson hit the bar twice for them before we equalised after a rocket of a shot from Brian Burrows deflected into the path of Mickey Gynn and he stuck it in the bottom corner in front of the West End.

We were fairly quiet as a group. I'd made a point of saying 'thanks' to Chris, but he wasn't his usual self, not with me at least.

"For what?" he said.

"The other night," I said, "at Leicester."

"Don't worry about it," he said.

I didn't know why he was being like that and I couldn't be arsed to ask him.

"I'm not worried," I told him.

I was going to tell him that I'd checked the Leicester Mercury for any report of an injured neanderthal and found none, in case he was concerned about it, which I guessed he wasn't.

Toward the end of the game, Bal sidled over to me and asked if he could have a word.

"What is it, mate?"

"Listen Steve," he said, "don't take this the wrong way, but on Monday night you said you'd split up with Sarah."

I sighed. I wasn't expecting this. In fact, it disappointed me, and I could see where this was going.

"We had a row, yeah," I shrugged.

"I'm sorry mate," he said. "I know you liked her."

'I liked her?' That's one way of putting it, I thought. Actually, I liked her a lot.

"Yeah, thanks," I said, and turned my attention to the game. City were back to their best in the second half and Cyril had just got up for a cross and put it wide.

"The thing is mate," Bal went on, "it's Barrath."

"What about him?"

"I know I'm asking a lot," he said, "but it's not for me. I'm trying to get him to be part of things, not stuck in the house all the time."

"That's great Bal," I said. "Really great. He's lucky to have a big brother like you."

"You're really going to make me ask, aren't you?"

"Ask what?" I said. I wasn't even sure why I was being such a dick, but I felt that there was something cold-blooded about what Bal was doing. He should at least suffer a little for doing the deed.

I felt like Jimmy at the end of Quadrophenia. My heart had been torn out and now my mates were picking over my bones.

"It's the biggest day ever," Bal said. He had turned his attention to the game now too. "It could be our only big day in history. I don't think it will ever happen again. And we'll be able to say that on the greatest day of our lives, we were there. All I'm asking is that you give my brother the chance to be there too."

I heard what he was saying. I had one of the very scarce spare tickets.

"There was no other way that he's getting a ticket from anywhere else," Bal pleaded, "not for love nor money."

I looked at him again. I knew I was supposed to do the right thing here. I could hear my mother telling me, 'You always do what's best, but sometimes you have to what's right.'

But I couldn't do it. It was Sarah's ticket.

"We had a row," I said, "we didn't split up."

"What?" Bal snapped. "That's not what you said on Monday night."

"Well, that was then," I said, "this is now."

Bal laughed and there was the same tone of disgust that my mum had laughed at me with.

"You know what, Steve?" he said, "we were all mates before we were anything else. Before we did school, before we had jobs, before the football, before we had girlfriends, before we were anything we were mates. And all it took was for one spoiled little rich-girl to flutter her eye-lashes and you've shit on all of us with no hesitation."

"It's not like that," I said.

"Yes it is," he snarled, "even now, after she's dumped you, like everyone knew she would, you still think she's coming back. You can't even think for yourself and you can't even see what's happening right in front of your eyes."

I took a deep breath.

"Tell me I'm lying. Tell me anything else," he said. "Tell me you sold it and made a profit. Or you gave it away to someone more deserving or more unfortunate than yourself. Or tell me you just set fire to it. Tell me anything. But don't tell me you won't sell it to my brother because you think she's coming back."

I let the question hang over us like poisonous gas as our friendship died from it.

"OK," Bal said. "I'll tell you what Steve? Fuck you. If I see you on fire, I won't even piss on you."

Then he was gone.

He went back to the lads, who looked to him hopefully, but he shook his head. Barrath was the only one who looked my way, but it was only a glance. Then they all made their way to the exit.

On the pitch, things fizzled out and the referee eventually put everyone out of their misery with the full time whistle.

< < < <   > > > >

If anyone was going to understand, it was Andy, but even he had disappeared at the end of the game.

But I had to speak to someone.

I rang his house from the Taj Mahal payphone and asked his mum to get him to ring me.

It was an hour later when the phone rang.

"Andy," I said.

"What's up?"

"What's going on, mate?"

"With what?"

I took a breath. "With us, mate, with everyone. Why am I the outcast all of a sudden?"

"Why are you asking me?" he said. "Every time I put a word in for you, you just keep digging a bigger hole. What was they supposed to do?"

"Well, I thought they might understand-"

"They understand that they're second-best, by a long way, as far as you're concerned. She says shit and you're on the shovel."

I didn't speak.

"I mean, we're in the F.A. Cup Final. We should've been celebrating this together, every step of the way, every game and every goal." He stopped there, deliberating whether or not to go on. "But you weren't there. And, like Bal says, 'we were mates before we were anything else', and that should count for something."

"Yeah, well," I said, "You won't have to worry about that anymore. You were right. You said it the night I met her. She wasn't just out of my league, she was playing a different game."

"You'll get back together," he said. "She's mad about you, for some reason."

"She's been cheating on me all along with the Audi Quattro guy," I said. "Lying and cheating from day one."

"Steve," Andy said, "Have you listened to yourself? Do you think she's that good an actress that she's fooled you for the last five months?"

"I was stupid. I must've be blind."

"Mate, you need to have a word with yourself, get some sleep or something. Get your head straight."

"Yeah, yeah, yeah, you're right," I said. "Thanks mate."

"Steve, don't be like tha-"

"I gotta go mate," I said, "don't worry about it, you're right, I'll just get my head straight. Catch you later, yeah?"

I put the phone down.

CHAPTER TWENTY-FOUR

Saturday 9th May 1987

The last home game of the season was a Wembley send-off party at Highfield Road and everyone was invited. The opposition were Southampton and sadly Brian Burrows, the best right-back in England, got injured and would miss the Final. This seemed to be the cruelest of fates as Burrows had done as much as anybody to get us there and because of one tackle, he was going to miss the biggest game of his career. It hurt just to imagine how he must be feeling.

The game ended one-all, but no one would remember the result, only the celebrations afterwards.

I didn't want to miss the occasion, but couldn't face any of my normal matchday routine and so I bought a ticket in the Sky Blue stand. I looked on as the referee blew the final whistle and thousands invaded the pitch. The players were mobbed and the fans rejoiced, as was normal at any end of season game, nevermind the last game before our first Cup Final appearance.

The police official in charge responded to the ultra-peaceful activity by sending policemen on horseback to charge around the pitch. This policing insanity caused mayhem and injury. The marauding horses caused stampedes of fans. At one time, there must have been thirty fans trapped in the actual goal net and more were running into them as a horse galloped through the crowd just yards away.

The next day I read that the need to 'protect the playing surface drove the decision', which considering it was the last game of the season, wasn't exactly a top priority. The only damage to the pitch I could see was the deep hoof prints of police horses.

I stayed in my seat, hating the insanity of the police but still trying to enjoy the achievement of the club, the players and the fans. It was then, for the first time, I began to think that my time doing this might be coming to an end. I'd always be a fan, City till I die, and, true, I was not in the most positive frame of mind what with recent events, but I definitely felt like my sense of belonging here was fading and there was nothing I could do about it.

What would replace it was not yet clear to me, but it was there in the shadows. I didn't know what it was, but I could already feel it pulling me away from here. Not forever. I'd still come to Highfield Road when I was a miserable old man in my sixties, God willing. But it was going to be different, probably only occasionally, maybe even rarely.

"We'll see," I told myself.

The crowd had amassed outside the tunnel and were demanding to see the players. I finally relented and wandered across the pitch as John Sillett appeared in the director's box and raised his arms for quiet.

Silence fell over the crowd as Sill made his speech. I wasn't close enough to hear him clearly, but I got the gist of it. 'Sill' was thanking the fans for their support and wished us all a great day out at Wembley. After more cheers, he raised his arms again and delivered his final words, "And this time next week, we'll be bringing the Cup back to Coventry!"

Highfield Road erupted.

As well as being the best manager we had ever had, and possibly the greatest men ever to walk the earth, John Sillett was the ultimate motivator and cheerleader, and he almost had me believing.

I was going to enjoy our big day out, but it wasn't going to be any more than that, was it?

CHAPTER TWENTY-FIVE

Wednesday 13th May

I stayed in the bedsit most of the week. Each night I tried to sleep but I ending up being awake all night with no one but my miserable self for company.

Even I didn't want to be around me anymore.

I wanted to shed my skin and be a new person, but instead I picked at the scars of my life and relived the mistakes I made, trying to see what I should have done differently and what I should do next.

There were two options that I came up with.

The first was to go to the wedding.

I seriously considered it, but it was too late to put things right. The damage was already done. It was too early to patch things up with my mum. Too late because I should've done it the first time and too late because she'd see it for what it was; an empty gesture driven by guilt.

Doing the right thing for the wrong reason wasn't going to cut it with my mum.

I would repair things though, and it would be difficult, but at least it would be fixed.

It was 2am on Wednesday morning when I decided on the second thing I had to do.

I fell asleep at six, woke again at nine, then got washed and dressed to go to the out.

< < < <   > > > >

I avoided Molly at the market by circling round her stall and keeping my head low. Nothing against her, but I just thought it best to avoid testing her loyalties.

The guy on the 'Computers and Games' stall was pleased to see me.

< < < <   > > > >

I decided to walk to Foleshill from the city centre.

The sun was out and the city was vibrant, flags and scarves and banners on every house and every car and every business. Part of me knew it was all fake, that when Coventry City were struggling in previous years, most people lost interest in them. I reminded myself that it was only football. As much as we loved the game, it was only a game.

And yet, besides a world war or two, what else had brought the people of this city together as one? It may just be football, but it had a power like nothing else.

I knocked on the front door and waited.

I guessed he'd be upstairs in his room.

He looked sheepish once he realised it was me. "What do you want?"

"Hi Barrath, can I come in."

He thought about it for a second, rolled his bottom lip into his mouth, then stepped aside.

We went to the kitchen. We didn't sit down. Barrath stared at the floor, leaving me to say what I had to say.

"We sold the games," I told him. "This is yours."

I put three twenty-pound notes on the table.

He raised his head slightly and eyed the money.

"You earned it," I said. "Can you make some more?"

He thought about it, or rather, he thought about the implications of doing something that involved me.

He nodded.

Money talks, bullshit walks.

"We'll need to buy some blank disks," he said, "I've got none left."

"I'm thinking four hundred," I said, "and a printer for the labels."

"Four hundred?" he asked, looking up for the first time. "You can sell four hundred games?"

"If you can make them I can."

"That means I get one-hundred and twenty quid?"

"No," I said, "I need to raise your cut from thirty pence a game to forty. So it'll be one-hundred and sixty quid. If that's OK with you?"

"I can live with that," he smiled.

"I'm thinking we could sell these games anywhere, everywhere. Every bloody market in the country will soon have a computer games stall and they're going to need our games, right?"

He nodded. I could almost hear the millions of thoughts clambering for attention in his head.

"We're going to need to new ideas and new games," I said. "If this computer game business is going to be big, then we need to get in on the ground floor, to be the first to market. You can be a pioneer. If you're up for the hard work, then the sky's the limit. That's what I think."

Barrath smiled. I liked the way he smiled too, not like someone who'd been flattered by friendly words, but someone who had been given a massive challenge they were ready to rise to. I liked that.

"So," I said. "Are we in business or what?"

"Yes, Steven," he said, "I want to do this more than anything in the world."

"Good," I said. "So do I."

Barrath's eyes widened to match his smile.

"I'm thinking we should be proper partners too, fifty-fifty on all decision making," I said, "And we'll need a name and a logo too. How about Rath87? What do you think?"

"I love it!"

"I'll leave the logo design to you. if that's alright?"

Barrath was alone with his thoughts for a moment, then burst into a fit of giggling laughter. "Thank you Steven," he said. "Thank you so much."

"Now that we're business partners, can you call me Steve?" I said.

"OK, Steve."

"And one more thing," I said and took the envelope from my pocket and put it next to the money. "And this is yours. You can open it when I've gone."

He stared at the envelope and put the palm of both hands to the side of his head.

"Is that what I think it is?" he said.

"That depends what you think it is," I smiled. "You just enjoy it."

Barrath looked at me and beamed a smile so wide I thought it would squeeze out all the tears he was holding back.

"Bal and the lads are driving down early Saturday morning to make a day of it," he told me.

I said, "That's great, it's going to be one hell of a day, isn't it."

It was time for me to leave.

"We can pick you up-"

I shook my head, "I'd love it, but I've already made plans, sorry, mate."

Barrath's chest deflated as he exhaled. "That's a shame," he said.

"Yeah," I said, "It is."

CHAPTER TWENTY-FIVE

Friday 15th May 1987

I'd intentionally put the TV on that Friday afternoon to watch the Coventry City Squad perform 'Go For It City' on Blue Peter. It was a traumatic horrifying event, but, like most car-crashes, I couldn't take my eyes off it.

Maybe this whole thing was a dream after all. What universe had I slipped into where Blue Peter has the Cov players miming to the most annoying song ever?

I was still recovering from this when there was a knock on the door. My heart sank. It could be any number of people, but none of them would be the bearers of good news. It was more likely to be a long queue of those intent on putting the boot in while I'm down.

I didn't even allow myself to consider the possibility of it being the one single person that I would be glad to see.

I knew it couldn't be, and it wasn't, but it was perhaps the closest thing.

"Hi," she said, "Can I come in?"

"Hi Danielle," I said, bowing as I waved her in. "Take a ticket and join the line."

"What line?" she said as she looked for somewhere to sit.

"Well, I guess you want to either give me a piece of your mind, an injunction order or a death threat," I smiled. "Or is this just a social call to check on my well-being?"

"Don't flatter yourself," she sighed. "You're not worth the ink of a death-threat, never mind the paper."

"Thanks for the pep talk," I said, "I'm feeling better already."

"I bet you're actually funny when your life's not turning to shit." She smiled and sat on the sofa. "Which is the real reason I'm here."

She looked like she was going somewhere nice, unless she'd gone through her wardrobe and chosen a maroon leather trousers and jacket set to visit my place. She really was an exceptionally beautiful person, if only she'd tell that to her face. Occasionally, a real smile or a laugh would reveal the identity of the person beneath the facade, but then it would leave and be replaced by what looked a lot like sadness. I couldn't help but be reminded of the ex-boyfriend that Danielle had broken up with and silently regretted.

And I might have been losing my mind, and how would I know if I was, but she seemed genuine.

"Would you like a drink?"

"Wine?"

I grimaced, "Sorry, I'm out of wine."

"What do you have?" she sighed.

I crossed the room, inspected the kitchen table and smelled the milk carton. "I have a dribble of milk and one tea-bag. I'm happy to split it with you, which is an honour because for most people I'd lie and say I've got nothing in."

"I'm touched, but I won't deprive you," she said. "Thanks anyway."

"Sorry about the mess," I said. It was amazing how much clutter can amass in a relatively short time when you no longer give a crap.

"It's fine," she said, "I've been in worse places, believe me."

"So what brings you here?" I said, which came out wrong. "I mean," I tried again, "thank you for doing this. Whatever this is."

I sat on the edge of the bed. Put my elbows on my knees and leant forward, ready to hit the fetal position if things got too depressing.

"I want to tell you about Greg and what he's been doing with my little sister," she said.

That conjured some fairly unpleasant images in my mind and my heart sank past rock bottom and kept going. "I don't really want to hear this."

"Well, you're going to hear it," she told me. "This is my sister we're talking about."

"Then spare me the graphic details," I moaned.

"I was the only one she told. Not because she trusted me or wanted to confide in me, just that I knew something was going on and I bugged her until she caved. And she made me promise never to tell a living soul until the day I die."

Just what I wanted to hear.

"So if I die today, it's all your fault."

"Well," I said, "for what it's worth, I hope you don't die today. Or any day this week come to that!"

"I'm touched," she said.

"I don't even know why she didn't tell you guys," I said. "I only know why she didn't tell me."

Danielle put her hand up to stop me. "Don't talk any more. You're embarrassing yourself. You really don't know anything, do you? And you haven't even managed to work out the basics."

I sighed and put my head in my hands. "Go on then," I sighed, "Tell me."

Greg just so happened to own a lorry cleaning company that wasn't making any money. When Sarah found out he was going to close it down, she asked if she could look into it. He said, 'Fine', you know how persuasive she can be. And, anyway, she saw it differently. She saw low-skilled jobs with a low-cost company and she saw an opportunity. So she talked Greg into starting Helping Hands and incorporating his company into it. Then she started talking to other companies and other organisations and she raised twenty-grand in capital to fund the company.

"And did you know her company's Mission Statement is 'To employ the unemployed and provide the first step to job ownership?' It's insane. Companies gave her money to start a company will never make a profit."

"It's very noble," I said.

"Noble? It's impossible!" she said. "But do you know she was most proud of?"

"I can hazard a good guess, but why don't you tell me?"

"She did it without our father finding out and interfering, without him putting a word in or influencing things, which is what he does," she said. "I think you've met our father. He's a bit controlling and overbearing sometimes, and Sarah hates it. She always wanted to do things on her own, without help and without quitting. That's what she wanted to do with 'Helping Hands' and she did it."

"Did she though? Did she do it by herself?"

"What do you mean?"

"How much of it was her, and how much was her boyfriend? Wasn't she just tagging along with him whilst he did all this? He owns the company, right?"

"He owned the failing company, they were making a loss, and she convinced him not to close it down. And then she turned it round, made them viable. She made it what it is, with his help."

"And they both lived happily ever after," I said. "I'm pleased for them. Glad I provided some comic-relief along the way."

"She went through hell, Steve, but she didn't quit. You have no idea how much it hurt her when she split up with Greg."

"Then why did she dump him?"

"She didn't dump him," she said. "He dumped her."

"Do you think I'm stupid? How would that ever happen?"

"Last December, before she'd even set eyes on your ugly mug," she said, "he went back to his ex. He promised her, on his life, that they were over, but he did it anyway. They got engaged. Sarah was devastated. It destroyed her. We wanted to kill him, but she told us all, and him, the company would go on as she planned and nobody and nothing was to get in the way of it."

I was confused. "So she kept working on 'Helping Hands' with him, knowing he was back with his-ex?"

"Yes," Danielle said, "and we were sworn to secrecy, not to tell dad."

"Your dad never knew?"

She shook her head. "We kept her secret."

I had no words. Was this real? Had I got it all wrong?

"You know what she told me?"

"What."

"That night she met you," Danielle said. "Sarah said it was the first night she hadn't cried since Greg dumped her."

CHAPTER TWENTY-SIX

Saturday 16th May 1987

On the morning of the game, I was determined to soak up as much of the great day as I could. I'd waited a long time for this and although I probably wasn't going to 'enjoy' it, I would savour the memories.

I'd been up all night trying to figure out if what Danielle had told me changed anything between me and Sarah, but I couldn't come up with anything. We'd broken up over our first row and that was more or less it. She'd lied to me and I'd been too dumb-struck to stand up for myself, so what was the point?

I was still awake by seven o'clock, so I got up and headed out.

There was only one place to go.

I wandered down Far Gosford Street and then took a left onto King Richards Street. The sky was mostly blue and Highfield Road looked particularly pleased with itself that morning.

The ground was empty and locked up.

The sign above the entrance said 'Welcome to Coventry City' and below that 'Main Stand Blocks K L M'.

I'd once seen a house for sale in this very street and begged mum to move, but she said she was happy where she was, thanks.

I peered through the gates at the corner of the pitch, the West Stand, the Club Shop and the posh foyer for the executive boxes next to the players' entrance. I'd seen the buses from most clubs arrive here over the years, sometimes with one or two of the greatest players in the world onboard. As kids, we could sneak through the gates and get players' autographs. We knew them all from our Panini stickers. Most of them were fine with us pestering them, some not so much.

I followed the footpath around the side of the club car park to the West End turnstiles block and followed the road into Thackhall Street. The block of turnstiles were the very same ones I had passed through with my dad for the first time in 1977. The rotten wooden gates were locked and there was broken glass embedded in the concrete on the roof. This was because, according to dad, back in the late 50s, him and two-hundred others stood on the roof of the West End toilet to watch City play Wolves in the Cup. The attendance had been 50,000, he reckoned.

I walked the length of the Sky Blue Stand, past the entrance to the Social Club, the ticket office, the steps leading down to the turnstiles and the entrance for the away fans' section.

From there, I could glimpse the Crow's Nest Terrace at the top of the old Spion Kop and the scoreboard at the centre.

Around the corner were the Kop turnstiles and toilet block and the famous sloping path that lead up to the terrace. Every game, at half-time, there would be over two-hundred blokes lined up to piss against the wall, creating a yellow stream that flowed down to flood the toilet itself.

At the top of the slope, Chris would insist on waiting beside the seven-foot high brick wall that separated us from away fans. Sooner or later, one of the away fans would place his plastic pint glass on top of the wall and Chris would take great pleasure in knocking it over them from our side. It was funny, even after all these years.

I loved this place with all my heart, and it was going to hurt to leave.

<< < < >> > >

I had a train ticket and walked to the station. The queues stretched as far as the eye could see. Many a song and can of beer was cracked open as we waited, but there was also a nervousness in the air. I blamed myself. After my travel exploits, I was definitely under some kind of curse; Bal's Viva breaking down at Stoke, the lift not turning up for Sheffield Wednesday and then the disaster that was Leeds. No sane person would want to go to a Cup game with me ever again.

I wasn't going to games next season. I needed to focus on something else, something more productive for my life in general, rather than a distraction. I had to harness the passion I felt for this football team and inject that into a new project, whatever that may be.

So today, our greatest day in history, was also going to be a farewell.

Three times the queue started moving and we stepped dutifully forward, each time getting closer. On the fourth attempt, I boarded the train. I took a seat amongst a family of five. Mum wore a sky blue woolly hat that had a cardboard cut-out of the Cup wrapped in silver foil pinned to it. She dished out the biscuits and cans of pop as soon as we sat down. The Bourbons and Custard Creams were devoured by a son and daughter no older than twelve, both in replica shirts, and a teenage girl trying her best not to be impressed by the size of the army she was part of, but taking it all in. Dad had the trusty egg-timer shirt from 1978, extra-large I'd say, the classic City scarf with the dark blue stripe in the white bar on a Sky Blue background, and a Mad-Hatter sized top hat in club colours.

What a family day-out, I thought. Something they would never forget.

When mum got up to order them all to huddle together for a photo, it was a pleasure for me to do the owners so she could be in the picture.

"Frame that one for the fireplace," I said as I handed back the camera.

Smiles all round. I don't think they could've been any happier.

Dad's tipple was a can of Carling. He offered me one and wouldn't take no for an answer.

"Cheers," I said and tapped my can to his. "Play up Sky Blues. I'm Steve."

"Kevin," he said, and raised his can. "The first of many, cheers!"

But no sooner had we put the cans to our lips that the train started to slow down. We were barely out of Coventry and were going direct to Wembley, so something wasn't right.

Obstacles on the track, was the reason given, but the train had already stopped by then. The curse has struck again.

The kids looked panicked, but Kevin calmed them. "Don't worry, they'll soon have it sorted. It's probably jealous Leicester fans! We'll clear the tracks ourselves if we have to."

I climbed the steps from Wembley train station and there, for the first time, I saw the Twin Towers.

We'd arrived.

I said my goodbyes to Kevin and his family and wished them all the best.

Thousands lined Wembley Way, more Coventry than Tottenham, a most beautiful sight indeed. Flags and scarves and smiling faces. We were here to enjoy the day.

I bought a hot-dog and took a seat on the wall up by the stadium. For years I'd watched this scene on TV, the camera up on the balcony looking down Wembley way. Usually it was Arsenal, Liverpool, Man Utd, or Everton fans flocking to the football Mecca, but today it was us. I couldn't help but beam with pride.

I started to remember all the low points that had preceded this event, the humiliating defeats in League and Cup, but I banished them immediately. This was not the time or the place.

I could've sat there all day, but it was already past two o'clock.

There was a buzz coming from inside the ground and I wanted to experience as much of being inside Wembley as I could.

I made my way to the top of the ramp and headed to the right. Our end was opposite the tunnel, (wc were to the left if I'd been watching on TV). The first gates I passed were crammed with City fans. There must've been a thousand at each one. I wasn't going to walk straight in, that was for sure, but I picked up the pace and moved to the outside of the wide walkway where there were less people.

That was when I saw him. He wasn't wearing colours, but he was a Spurs fan. There was something about him that marked him out as a Londoner. Like me he was making his way around the stadium to his gate, but unlike me, he seemed too interested in other people. He had his hands tucked into a Harrington jacket and his eyes darted constantly from left to right and back again.

I watched him and steered my path away from his.

I knew I was over-reacting. There'd never been any crowd trouble at a Cup Final before. But knowing that it wasn't 'the done thing' didn't mean it would never happen, first time for everything and all that. Then his eyes caught mine and made a B-line for me. He was twenty-yards away and I couldn't even veer away as he'd do the same and cut me off.

He nodded his chin to greet me and gave a non-committal nod back and tried to up my pace even more, but then I realised the nod was a distraction and he was waving me over to him with his left hand. His right hand was still inside his jacket pocket.

I nodded my head forward to tell him I had to get somewhere and he shook his head.

"Hey mate!" he said, ten yards away from me, his left hand waving for me to come closer.

I stopped and turned to face him but edged sideways half a step, then again. "You alright mate?" I said, "I'm running late, as it goes."

"Yeah, yeah, me too," he said.

Five yards away.

He's pulling his right hand out of his coat pocket, but it's stuck and won't come free.

I'm thinking, Knife! Knife! He has a knife! This is just a ploy to get close enough to stab me.

This is it. I'm going to get stabbed outside Wembley Stadium on Cup Final Day.

What 'never happens', is happening to me now.

I step sideways again, watching his hand.

I'll do what I have to do if I see any metal in his hand, but what if he's too quick?

What then?

But now he's stood right in front of me. I can smell the beer on him.

"Mate," he says.

No time to think as his right hand frees itself from his jacket pocket and he thrusts it at me. I grab it, but he grabs mine first. I feel his empty palm in mine. No knife.

My knees could hardly hold me up.

He shook my hand with two solid pumps.

"Just wanted to say good luck, yeah?" he said.

"Yeah," I said, "Thanks. You too."

My heart was racing. I wasn't sure what I just said.

"Let the best team win, eh?" he said.

"Yeah, yeah, absolutely," I said, "Thanks. Thanks."

"No problem, mate," he smiled and let go of my hand. "Take care of yourself, yeah, and have a safe journey home."

"Yeah, you too."

<<<< >>>>

The crowding at my gate wasn't as bad as others had been and within fifteen minutes, I was through the turnstile and into the concourse beneath the sacred terraces. City fans were still swarming everywhere and all I wanted to do was to climb the last few steps and take in the view of the pitch, the Twin Towers above and the one-hundred thousand people gathered inside.

I checked my ticket again and found my pen. There was another queue as they checked tickets and we were patted down, but by this time, people were getting impatient. To be so close and to be told to wait was getting to be too much.

I took a breath, resisted the urge to look at my watch again, and waited until it was my turn to step forward.

Within minutes, I'd showed my ticket, got patted down, waved through and told to 'enjoy the game'.

There were twelve steps that lay before me. Twelve more steps and I would complete the journey that for me had been ten years. For the club, it had been one hundred and four years. But here we were. The volume of the noise hit me. The songs and roar of the crowd echoing in the concourse were the loudest I'd ever heard, literally drowning out my thoughts.

I climbed the steps and again my mind went back to 1977, walking up to the Sky Blue terrace and seeing that beautiful green pitch for the first time. This green pitch, which was just as beautiful, was where England had won the World Cup, the goal at our end was where Geoff Hurst had scored the fourth goal, where Trevor Brooking had scored his header to win the Cup for West Ham in 1980, where City favourite Tommy Hutchison had scored for both sides in 1981 and Ricardo Villa had scored one of the greatest Cup Final goals ever in the replay, where Liverpool beat Everton last year to win the double. I wondered whether there'd be any magical moments here today. Whether there'd be any goals that people would be watching forty years from now. This place was the most historic stadium in the world. Today was one of the most famous games. The FA Cup Final was watched all over the planet. This was history in the making. And I hoped we wouldn't lose by too many.

There must have been forty thousand Cov fans and all of them waving flags, banners, scarves. It was an incredible sight, unbelievable despite my imagining it for weeks, still fantastical, unreal. My eyes tried to take it all in, to commit every detail to memory.

My pen was already full. I found a spot near the back beside the fence.

When I'd watched on TV over the years, I always enjoyed picking out the banners in the crowd and I did the same now, but from standing on the same terrace. There was one in the design of a box of England's Glory matchbox, with a picture of John Sillett and George Curtis at its centre in place of the ship. Another was simply in our club colour with the club badge at the centre, but it was huge, the size of the penalty area at least. It rippled on top of the crowd and I wondered how they could see from beneath it. 'Send the Cup to Coventry', 'Go For It City' and 'Sky High City' were all popular and there was even one of an elephant having sex with a cockerel.

"Ladies and Gentlemen, please stand for the FA Cup hymn, Abide With Me."

The song was another rite of passage and I sang with all my heart as much as I ever had for any City song.

Time was running out. In minutes, the buildup would be over, the best part, and the game would begin and with it would come the reality that we'd done well to get this far, but it was never going to be our day. The biggest Lesson One of all time.

When the players came out of the tunnel, someone twenty rows in front of us put their banner up and we couldn't see a thing.

The guy next to me, who was my age, had bought in a copy of The Times newspaper and had been tearing the pages into squares the size of playing cards.

"Ticker tape," he'd explained to me.

"Mario Kempes!" I'd said.

He smiled and nodded. "That's right!"

I offered to tear some pages for him and in no time, he had a wad of paper the size of a house brick.

But now, the moment we had waited for, was obscured by some idiots with a flag.

"Put your flag down!" my new friend was screaming. "Put your bloody flag down you idiots!"

"Oi!" someone yelled, "Put your flag down!"

"I've waited years for this," my new friend said and threw his wad of ticker tape at the flag bearer. The wad flew through the air and remained intact to strike the intended target squarely on the back of the head.

He turned round to a sea of angry faces and lowered his banner.

The players, oblivious to the restriction of our view, had continued their walk and were amassing on the halfway line for the Royal introduction.

We were in full voice now. Singing as one and easily out-singing the Tottenham fans, most of whom had all seen all this before.

"I think we can do this," said the lad next to me.

"I don't think so," I said, smiling. "Hopefully we can give them a good game, but realistically-"

"I have a feeling about this ever since Stoke," he said, "You'll see."

"I do hope you're right," I said.

On the pitch, players were introduced to someone important and hands were shaken and heads bowed slightly and we started a roar that grew and grew and grew and then the players broke away and my eardrums shattered as the roar exploded. Our players running to our side, Spurs going to their end. Players applauded us, we applauded back and the roar grew again.

The band marched off the pitch and Kilcline met Richard Gough and the referee on the halfway line.

Tracksuit tops were discarded, the kick-about-balls were kicked off the pitch, and the players wandered into their starting positions.

"Here we go, here we go, here we go-oh!" we sang, not the most inventive song to usher in the biggest game in history, but it perfectly matched our happy-go-lucky mood.

It was all going too quickly. Soon it would be over. My last match would soon be a memory.

Tottenham kick-off.

We get the ball and Houchen goes forward with it. He wins a throw-in down there end, but we lose possession.

So far, so good.

A song goes out, all of us singing, "City score, City score, if you get one you'll get more, you'll see our assembly when we get to Wembley, so score, City score."

Tottenham play it around on the halfway line and McGrath knocks the ball off Hoddle's toe which the ref thinks is against the rules and gives Spurs a free kick

Hoddle himself takes it and puts the ball into our box, but we deal with it. Keith Houchen heads it away, but it lands at Clive Allen's feet. My heart is in my mouth, but Allen doesn't control it and Mickey Gynn clears the ball upfield.

It goes straight to Chris Waddle.

Greg Downs is there, stopping him from going inside, and when Waddle goes to cross it Greg has it covered, but then Waddle cuts it back and gets to the bi-line. Downs has been royally mugged and Waddle has all the time in the world to pin point his cross to the near post.

It looks dangerous. Clive Allen is perfectly positioned in the six-yard box and, as the saying goes, he doesn't miss from there. The ball flashes past Oggy and hits the back of the net.

Tottenham are one-nil up.

There was a joyous roar from the other end of the ground and we stood in silence.

"Not even two minutes gone," someone said behind me.

I looked around at the faces of my fellow fans, then bowed my head so I didn't have to watch the flag waving Spurs fans celebrating.

When I looked up, nothing had changed. Cov fans were still smiling but now in shock, stunned by a slap in the face. There were no flags waving any more. No singing for the time-being.

It was time for a brief prayer. And I prayed for a goal, just one. It didn't matter to me if Spurs scored six now, as long as we scored one and we, Coventry City, would show Wembley, and the world, a celebration like it had never seen before.

Just one goal. If that wasn't too much to ask.

"Plenty of time left," the guy next to me said, "this ain't over by a long shot."

I was about to say, 'I think it is mate', but held it back. I didn't want to be the one who destroyed this incredible optimism, time, tide and the second and third goals would do that soon enough, so I nodded in agreement and gave it a "C'mon City!"

A few other cries went up and the City roar began to rumble, then the guy next to me said, "Do you know her?"

"Say again," I shouted. I lean a little closer to him. I hadn't heard him right.

"That girl," he shouted, "do you know her?"

He was pointing at the pen to our left, down by where the banner had been raised a few minutes ago, but on the other side of the fence.

"She seems to know you," he said.

I looked, but all I could see were the backs of a thousand people's heads and no one moving.

Then someone raised an arm, waving with big wide pendulum swings, the kind that are used for drawing attention. She was standing on the crash barrier, her other hand holding the fence for balance.

The waving arm had a huge Adidas logo and she was crying.

"Oh my God!" I said. "Sarah. My Adidas angel."

Was it her? How could it be?

Was it someone who looked like her? That just wasn't even possible?

I could almost hear her. In fact, I was sure I could. She was calling my name.

I pushed my way toward her, pushing past people, staying close to the fence and looking for her for what felt like way too long.

Then she was there.

"Sarah!" I shouted.

She pushed her fingers through the fence and I wrapped them in mine.

"I found you!" she sobbed, "I found you!"

"Don't cry," I said, "Sarah, please don't cry."

She pressed her face to the fence and we kissed. Her lips tasted of cherry and tears. Nothing ever tasted so sweet.

"I'm so sorry," she kept saying.

"How did you get in?" I asked.

"Andy gave me his ticket," she said. "He turned up at my house this morning. Told me I was stupid and took me to your bedsit, but you weren't there."

"He did?" I gasped. I couldn't believe it. But then, of course, I could. It was Andy all over, thinking of everyone else before himself.

She nodded and wiped away a tear. "I didn't think I'd ever find you," she said, "I've been looking for hours."

I smiled so hard I thought my jaw would break, my heart was already melting in tears of my own.

"I'm sorry I lied to you Steve, I should've trusted you, but I never cheated on you."

"I know," I said, "I know and I'm sorry too."

She looked up at the top of the fence and I thought the same thing that she did.

I let go of her hands and reached up, got a grip on the fence, and began to climb. Cheers went up as I reached the top and I could hear a steward barking at me to get down, but I had to concentrate on the tricky bit of swinging each leg over the spikes without slipping. I didn't think of the consequences and, with a degree of elegance that impressed on-lookers and myself, I crossed over and dropped to the ground beside her.

I held her so tight and she clung to me. As we swayed and breathed her in and our tears met on our cheeks and we shared our heaven where the wildest dreams come true.

"Don't ever leave me," I told her.

"I won't," she promised, "not ever."

I kissed her again and again.

"Come on," she said. "Shall we watch the match? I still think we can do this."

CHAPTER TWENTY SEVEN

AFTERWARDS

I won't bore you with what happened on the pitch, I'm sure you've seen it by now. Brilliant wasn't it. I'm biased of course, but it was the greatest FA Cup Final ever.

The word everyone used to describe it was 'unbelievable' but to me it was the most believable thing I'd ever seen. It was real, it was us, for once. We won the Cup.

If I ever get chance I'd like to thank all of the players and staff from that season because their hard work and belief in each other made an impossible dream come true. And it absolutely changed my life, hand on heart, it made me realise that our wildest dreams are achievable.

Andy was waiting for us outside the stadium.

That was quite a celebration.

He'd watched the game in a packed bar outside Wembley, but he wasn't alone. He'd picked up a stray along the way and seemed quiet happy about it.

The next day me and Sarah spent the day in the city centre for the open-top bus parade. It was her that suggested that we should start at the Wyken Pippin and follow the bus in to town and it was an inspired idea.

We stood on the same spot that we had waited for the landlord of the Green Man to pick us up, the location of our greatest despair.

Seeing the bus, with the players and the Cup, was an amazing experience that those there would never forget.

We followed the crowd as the bus crawled along at walking pace. It was like every Coventry carnival parade was happening all at once. It took hours and we loved every minute.

Outside the council buildings, the players on parade on the balcony, and almost every person from Coventry was there, or so it seemed.

As the players retreated for a well-earned rest, and no doubt more liquid refreshments, which they kind of deserved, we stayed and watched the crowds disperse.

We were sat on the steps of the Natwest Bank, Sarah in my arms.

"There must've been fifty-thousand people here today," I said, "maybe more."

Sarah nodded.

"Football," I said. "There's nothing else that can bring people together. These people can achieve anything when they're united like this."

< < < <   > > > >

That following Friday night we went to The Pilot.

Sarah grabbed my arm as we stepped in the door and I scanned the room.

I held the door open for Andy and he had a protective arm round Danielle. They'd hardly been separated since he'd turned up at Sarah's house on the morning of the Cup Final. Watching the match in a bar with Danielle had made giving his ticket away a little more bearable, but he still would've done it. Andy always did what's right, not what's best. Maybe that's why Danielle hadn't let him out of her sight ever since.

The mini-bus lads were there. Gary, Dave, Keith, everyone.

Naturally, we were in high spirits, introductions were made and I bought the first round.

My head was pleasantly spinning as drank and relived the Cup Final day, each taking turns to tell tales of our shared experience.

For as long as we live we'll never forget what supporting Coventry City meant to us on that day, but as I listened to the stories I realised that already the details were fading in the memory. I wanted to go back and relive it again and again.

And I hoped that maybe we could do it again, although, we'll probably have to wait 104 years again.

Sarah turned and whispered in my ear her hair brushing against my face. "Where is he?"

I shook my head. "Don't know. I'll ask, later."

She lost her smile for a few seconds and looked around. "Maybe he didn't come home?"

She needn't have worried, just ten minutes later the doors swung open and he walked in.

"Gerry!" Sarah screamed.

He recognised her straight away and she flew up to him, put her arms around him.

"You made it back!" she shouted.

"I did," he smiled. "No danger."

"Get you're hands off my girlfriend!" I told him.

Sarah let him go and as he stood at the bar he slipped his hand into a coat pocket.

"Uh-oh," Sarah smiled.

Gerry smiled, "Calm down boys and girls, I feel a song coming on."

And with a quick swig of his magic singing fluid, Gerry sang.

"If I were a football player, for Coventry City!

All the pretty girls, would always be with me….."

Thanks for reading

I hope you enjoyed She Wore
A Sky Blue Ribbon. I
enjoyed writing it and
reliving the adventures of
the 1987 Cup Run which I
was fortunate enough to
witness.

I would like to say again
my thanks to those the
players who made it happen,
from those of us who were
privileged to be carried
along with you.

Especially for George, John
and Cyril.

Very Special Thanks

I am exceptional thankful for the contribution of the following wonderful people

Jack, Mum and dad, Jason Beresford, Chris Twigger, Caroline J Clarke, Jenny Jones, Rob Summerfield, Nigel C, fish, MyFootballBooks, Dean Nelson, Deb Nelson, SkyBluesTalk, The Sky Blue Hub, Mark Hornby, Chris Evans at The Set Pieces, Chris in Block 22 and so many others, thank you.

About the Author

Paul Gilbert lives in Bedworth with his wife and his dog Ricoh. He is a season ticket holder in Block 22 and likes to talk about the City of today and yesterday

You can contact him at

swasbr87@gmail.com

or

@SkyBlueGilly on Twitter

If you enjoyed the book please leave a review which will help others find it.

Special thanks

for the Artwork **samiaakhter1**

and for the Cover Design **thekidonmars**

Take care

PUSB

Paul

Edition One January 2002
ISBN 9798797538851
PUSB

Printed in Great Britain
by Amazon

85938069R00180